Beyond the Ice Wall: Earth's FInal Frontier

Cassiel E. Nox

Published by Cassiel E. Nox, 2024.

BEYOND THE ICE WALL: EARTH'S FINAL FRONTIER

First edition. September 19, 2024.

Copyright © 2024 Cassiel E. Nox.

ISBN: 979-8227466754

Written by Cassiel E. Nox.

Table of Contents

Preface...1

- Introduction to Mysteries Beyond the Ice Wall.................3

- Embracing the Unknown 6

- Ice Wall: The Veil of Secrets.................................8

The Enigmatic Ice Wall 10

- Shrouded in Ice and Mystery.................................. 11

- Frozen Barriers of Perception 13

- Unveiling the Unseen Boundary................................ 15

Mythical Realms Beyond 17

- Echoes of Forgotten Lands 19

- Veiled in Myth and Legend................................... 21

- Secrets of Ancient Civilizations.............................. 23

Shadows of the Unknown.. 25

- Alien Intrigue at the Earth's Edge 27

- Whisperings of Otherworldly Beings........................... 29

- Unearthly Connections to the Ice Wall........................ 31

Concealed Truths and Covert Operations........................ 33

- Uncovering Hidden Expeditions 35

- Shadows of Deception in the Ice 37

- Government Secrets Beyond the Wall........................... 39

Unraveling the Ice's Mysteries 41

- Scientific Enigmas of Antarctica............................. 43

- Icy Riddles and Climate Conundrums........................... 45

- Challenging the Ice Wall's Illusions.......................... 47

Chronicles from the Frigid Frontier 49

- Frozen Tales of Exploration 51

- Descending into the Unknown................................. 53

- Journals of Ice Wall Voyagers................................ 55

Life's Unseen Domain 58

- Alien Ecosystems Beyond the Barrier.......................... 60

- Mysteries of Otherworldly Civilizations....................... 62

- Unveiling the Enigmatic Life Beyond.......................... 64

Impact on Earth's Paradigms...................................66

- Rupturing Reality's Perceptions 68
- Ice Wall's Revelation on Humanity 71
- Shifting the Earth's Axis of Understanding 73
Unveiling the Veil of Reality 74
- Quest for Truth Beyond the Ice Wall 76
- Truth Seekers in the Frozen Unknown 78
- The Everlasting Search for Enlightenment 80
Epilogue: Shadows in the Perpetual Ice 82
- Reflecting on Trails of Ice and Shadows 84
- Beyond the Veil of Ice: Forever Mysteries 86
- Embracing the Eternal Journey 88
Appendix: Further Explorations of the Unknown 90
- Resonating Echoes of the Ice Wall 92
- Prolonging the Quest for Knowledge 93
- Beyond the Book's Final Pages 95
Glossary of Enigmatic Terms 97
- Definitions Shrouded in Mystery 99
- Unveiling the Lexicon of Secrets 101
- Deciphering the Ice Wall's Tongue 103
Index of Unseen Realms 105
- Navigating the Enigmatic Extents 107
- Guiding Through the Shadows 109
- Illuminating the Darkened Ice 111

Beyond the Ice Wall: Earth's Final Frontier

The Ice Wall, a colossal expanse of frozen terrain that encircles Antarctica, has long been a source of fascination and speculation for explorers, scientists, and conspiracy theorists alike. Stretching for thousands of miles, this imposing ice barrier has sparked countless rumors and legends about what lies beyond its frigid embrace.

According to some theories, the Ice Wall is a physical boundary beyond which lies uncharted territory and even entirely new worlds. Stories of lost civilizations hidden beneath the ice have circulated for centuries, with some claiming that ancient peoples once thrived in the harsh Antarctic landscape before disappearing without a trace.

In more recent times, the Ice Wall has been at the center of conspiracy theories alleging government cover-ups and covert operations. Whispers of secret military installations, extraterrestrial encounters, and hidden research facilities abound, painting a portrait of a region shrouded in mystery and intrigue.

Scientists, too, have been drawn to the enigmatic allure of the Ice Wall, seeking to unlock its secrets and understand the forces that shape our planet. From studies of ice cores containing ancient air bubbles to investigations of the unique ecosystems that thrive in this extreme environment, researchers continually push the boundaries of knowledge and discovery to unravel the mysteries of Antarctica's icy perimeter.

With advances in technology, such as satellite imagery and remote sensing tools, scientists have been able to delve deeper into the secrets of the Ice Wall. They have uncovered evidence of ancient volcanic activity, preserved beneath layers of ice, hinting at a tumultuous geological past that shaped the formation of the vast ice sheet we see today.

Recent expeditions to the Ice Wall have revealed surprising findings about the region's biodiversity. Contrary to widespread belief, Antarctica is not a barren wasteland, but a vibrant ecosystem teeming with life. From microscopic organisms that thrive in icy waters to massive whales that migrate through the Southern Ocean, the Antarctic environment is a delicate balance of resilience and adaptation.

As we embark on a journey 'Beyond the Ice Wall,' we are met with a tapestry of tangled truths and interesting mysteries. Behind the veil of ice and snow lies a realm that challenges our understanding of the world, inviting us to question what we think we know and explore the edges of human knowledge. Join me as we venture into the unknown, navigating the icy expanse of Antarctica to uncover the secrets hidden beneath the surface of Earth's last frontier.

Preface

As we venture further beyond the Ice Wall, the stark beauty of the frozen landscape gives way to a sense of awe-inspiring vastness. The icy expanse stretches endlessly before us, a testament to the raw power of nature and the resilience of life in the harshest of environments.

In this desolate realm, where temperatures plummet to unimaginable lows and winds howl with unearthly fury, ancient mysteries lurk beneath the surface. Tales of lost civilizations and mythical creatures echo through the frozen wasteland, hinting at a truth far stranger than anything we could ever imagine.

Legends speak of a hidden world beyond the Ice Wall, a realm of perpetual twilight where time seems to stand still. Whispers of ancient temples and forgotten cities drift through the icy air, beckoning us to unravel their secrets and unlock the mysteries of a bygone era.

As we press on, the landscape shifts and changes around us, revealing glimpses of a haunting and beautiful world. Crystalline ice formations glisten in the feeble light, their intricate patterns speaking of craftsmanship long lost to the annals of time. Adapted to extreme conditions, strange creatures watch us from the shadows, their eyes filled with wisdom that transcends mere survival.

Reality blurs in this realm beyond the Ice Wall, and time loses meaning. We find ourselves caught in a liminal space where the boundaries between the known and the unknown dissolve. The fabric of existence seems to warp and shift, drawing us deeper into infinite possibility and unfathomable wonder.

And so we journey on, guided by a curiosity that knows no bounds and a determination that knows no limits. Beyond the Ice Wall lies a world waiting to be discovered, a world of mystery and magic that defies all reason and understanding. As we stand on the threshold of this frozen frontier, a sense of anticipation fills our hearts, for we know that the secrets of this uncharted realm are ours to uncover.

As we venture deeper into the frozen wasteland, the air around us crackles with otherworldly energy. Shadows dance on the icy landscape, their movements hinting at a presence beyond our sight. Whispers of long-forgotten voices drift on the wind, their words a cryptic riddle that teases the edges of our understanding.

The ice seems to pulse with a life all its own, shimmering with a faint, ghostly light that tricks the mind. Shapes and forms flit in and out of existence, teasing us with glimpses of the surreal and the impossible. In this frozen realm, where time bends and reality warps, we are no longer sure what is real and what is illusion.

And yet, despite the strangeness and the uncertainty, a sense of wonder fills our hearts. We are explorers in a world untouched by civilization, pioneers in a land where the laws of nature seem to have been rewritten. Every step we take leads us further into the unknown, deeper into a mystery that defies all logic and reason.

As we push forward, driven by a thirst for knowledge and a hunger for discovery, the secrets of the Ice Wall unfold before us. Ancient ruins loom on the horizon, their crumbling walls whispering of a civilization long lost to the ravages of time. Strange symbols adorn the stones; their meaning is lost to all but the most dedicated arcane scholars.

And in the distance, a faint glow beckons us onward, a glimmer of light in the darkness that promises untold secrets waiting to be revealed. We steel ourselves for what lies ahead, knowing that we are on the cusp of uncovering truths that will shake the very foundations of our understanding of the world.

- Introduction to Mysteries Beyond the Ice Wall

In the vast icy expanse of the Antarctic, the enigmatic Ice Wall, serving as Earth's last frontier, is shrouded in mystery. Beyond this imposing barrier lies a realm of untold secrets and uncharted territories waiting to be discovered by those brave enough to venture into the unknown.

The Ice Wall, a towering and seemingly impenetrable structure of ice, has long captivated the imaginations of explorers, scientists, and conspiracy theorists alike. Its sheer magnitude and enigmatic presence evoke a sense of wonder and curiosity, beckoning intrepid souls to uncover the truths hidden within its frozen depths.

As we delve into the mysteries beyond the Ice Wall, we face questions that challenge our understanding of the world. What lies beyond this icy boundary? Are there ancient civilizations waiting to be unearthed or otherworldly beings watching from the shadows? The allure of the unknown pulls at our core, driving us to seek answers in the icy wilderness beyond.

Join us on a journey into the heart of the Antarctic, where reality blends with myth and legend, and the line between truth and fiction becomes blurred. Step across the threshold of the Ice Wall and into a realm where secrets lie buried beneath layers of ice and snow, waiting to be revealed to those daring enough to uncover them.

As we embark on this quest for knowledge and enlightenment, we must heed the warnings of those who have gone before us. The Ice Wall is not merely a physical barrier; it symbolizes the mysteries that lurk at the edges of our understanding, challenging us to expand our perception of the world and embrace the unknown with open minds and fearless hearts.

The journey beyond the Ice Wall is fraught with danger and uncertainty, but it is also a gateway to a realm of infinite possibility and discovery. As we stand on the precipice of the unknown, we are reminded that the most incredible adventures await those willing to step beyond the boundaries of what is known and venture into the uncharted territories of the human spirit.

Venturing forth, one cannot help but feel the weight of history pressing down upon them, a silent reminder of all that has come before and all that is yet to be revealed. The Ice Wall is a sentinel of time, its frozen facade whispering tales of ages long past and prophecies of futures yet to unfold. It is a place where the boundaries of reality blur, and the veil between worlds grows thin.

As explorers brave the harsh elements and treacherous terrain, they are drawn deeper into the mysteries hidden within the icy labyrinth beyond the Ice Wall. Ancient artifacts and strange anomalies dot the landscape, hinting at a forgotten history and truth waiting to be unearthed. The air hums with energy, charged with the possibility of revelation and transformation.

In the shadows of towering ice cliffs, whispers of a lost civilization echo through the frozen landscape, beckoning those who dare to listen. Myths and legends intertwine with the stark reality of the Antarctic, blurring the lines between fact and fiction. Each step forward unveils new mysteries, each discovery leading further down the winding path of exploration and discovery.

As the sun dips below the horizon, casting the icy world into twilight, a sense of awe and wonder fills the hearts of those standing on the unknown's threshold. What lies beyond the Ice Wall remains an enigma, a puzzle waiting to be solved by those who possess the courage and curiosity to seek the truths hidden within the frozen expanse.

As the intrepid explorers venture deeper into the icy wilderness, they notice subtle changes in the surrounding environment. Strange symbols etched into the ice suggest a language long forgotten. Ancient ruins peek out beneath layers of snow, hinting at a civilization that predates any known to modern history. The very fabric of reality seems to warp and twist in this frozen realm, leaving the explorers to question the very nature of their existence.

Strange phenomena occur as the expedition presses on, with whispers of voices on the wind and shadows flitting past in the periphery of vision. The veil between worlds grows thinner, allowing glimpses into realms beyond human comprehension. Some team members report visions of creatures that defy description, while others claim to see glimpses of their past lives playing out before them.

Yet, despite the myriad challenges and dangers confronting them, the explorers press on, driven by an insatiable thirst for knowledge and a deep-seated curiosity about the mysteries beyond the Ice Wall. Each discovery brings them closer to unlocking the secrets of this enigmatic realm, but also raises new questions about the world's true nature and humanity's place within it.

As the expedition reaches the heart of the frozen wilderness, a sense of anticipation and trepidation hangs heavy in the air. They stand on the brink of a discovery that could forever change the course of history, their hearts pounding with excitement and fear at what lies ahead. The Ice Wall looms before them, a sentinel of mystery and wonder, daring them to take the ultimate step into the unknown.

- Embracing the Unknown

A world of limitless possibilities and unknowns lies in the depths of uncertainty. Embracing the unknown is a daring journey into the uncharted territories of our existence, where the familiar gives way to the strange and the known transforms into the enigmatic.

This is a call to step out of your comfort zone and embrace the unconventional. Embracing the unknown is a testament to the human spirit's insatiable thirst for knowledge and discovery, pushing boundaries and challenging perceptions.

Humans have always been drawn to the enigma of the unknown, seeking to make sense of the inexplicable and to shed light on the darkest corners of our existence. From ancient civilizations exploring uncharted lands to modern scientists delving into the depths of the cosmos, the impulse to unravel mysteries has driven our evolution as a species.

At the heart of embracing the unknown lies a deep curiosity, a thirst for understanding that transcends the constraints of our limited perspective. It is a recognition that there is more to the world than meets the eye, that beyond our current knowledge lies a vast expanse of unexplored territory waiting to be discovered.

Embracing the unknown is not without its challenges. It requires courage to step into the realm of uncertainty, to confront the fear of the unfamiliar and the anxiety of not knowing what lies ahead. Yet, in these moments of discomfort and unease, we often find the most significant opportunities for growth and transformation.

Faced with uncertainty, there is beauty in persisting to understanding, in the quest for truth that transcends the limitations of our current knowledge. It is a reminder that our journey through life is defined not by the answers we find, but by the questions we ask and the willingness to embark on a voyage of discovery into the unknown.

So, let us embrace the unknown with open hearts and curious minds, for it is in the embrace of uncertainty that we unlock the true potential of our existence. By daring to explore the uncharted territories of our world and our minds, we may discover previously unimaginable truths and illuminate the path toward a future filled with endless possibilities and infinite wonder.

A profound transformation occurs in this realm of uncertainty, where the known and the unknown converge. It is a space where our preconceived notions are challenged, our beliefs are tested, and our understanding of the world is reshaped in ways we could never have imagined. As we navigate through the shadows of ambiguity and ambiguity, we are reminded of the vastness of existence and the boundless potential within each of us.

Embracing the unknown is not just a journey of discovery, but a journey of self-discovery. It is unveiling the layers of our own perceptions, beliefs, and biases and confronting them with courage and humility. It invites us to step into the vulnerability of not knowing, embrace the discomfort of uncertainty, and welcome the transformative power of the unknown.

In this space of uncertainty, we are confronted with the limitations of our understanding and the vastness of the mysteries surrounding us. It is a humbling experience, a reminder of our humanity in the face of the infinite expanse of the universe. Yet, it is also a moment of liberation, a release from the constraints of our minds, and a stepping stone towards a more profound connection with the world.

So, let us venture boldly into the unknown with open hearts and curious minds, ready to embrace the mysteries that lie ahead. For it is in the embrace of uncertainty that we discover the true essence of our being, the unlimited potential that lives within us, and the boundless wonders that await us on the other side of fear.

- Ice Wall: The Veil of Secrets

As scholarly interest in the Ice Wall intensified, a team of intrepid explorers embarked on a daring expedition to probe its icy perimeter. Equipped with state-of-the-art technology and unwavering determination, they ventured into the depths of Antarctica, drawn by the allure of uncovering the secrets hidden within the frozen fortress.

The journey to the Ice Wall was fraught with challenges, as the unforgiving terrain tested the team's resolve at every turn. Bitter winds howled across the icy expanse, threatening to engulf them in a swirling vortex of whiteout conditions. Yet, undeterred by the harsh environment, the explorers pressed on, driven by a thirst for knowledge and a sense of adventure that burned brightly within their hearts.

A sense of awe swept over the team as they closed in on the looming silhouette of the Ice Wall. The sheer scale of the barrier was staggering, stretching as far as the eye could see in both directions, a monolithic presence that seemed to defy all logic and reason. Towering spires of ice rose majestically into the sky, their crystalline surfaces shimmering in the pale light of the Antarctic sun.

Drawing closer to the Ice Wall, the explorers detected a strange energy humming in the air, a palpable sense of anticipation that tingled along their skin. The very fabric of reality seemed to shimmer and warp near the barrier, hinting at the possibility of hidden dimensions and unseen forces at play. It was like the Ice Wall was a gateway to another realm, a threshold between the known and the unknown.

As they set up camp at the base of the Ice Wall, the explorers began their meticulous observations and measurements, eager to unlock the secrets that lay dormant within its icy embrace. Core samples were extracted from the frozen surface, revealing ancient layers of ice that held within them a record of Earth's tumultuous history. Each stratum told a story of climatic changes and catastrophic events, offering a glimpse into the past and a warning for the future.

But the genuine revelations came when the explorers stumbled upon a series of strange symbols etched into the ice; intricate patterns seemed to pulse with otherworldly energy. These enigmatic markings defied all attempts at decipherment; their meaning was shrouded in mystery and speculation. Were they a message from an ancient civilization, a code left behind by a long-forgotten race? Or were they the product of a more sinister force, a warning of dangers lurking beyond the Ice Wall?

As the expedition delved deeper into the heart of the Ice Wall, they uncovered evidence of advanced technology buried beneath the frozen surface. Strange artifacts of unknown origin lay scattered amidst the ice, their purpose and function a tantalizing enigma. Could these relics be remnants of a lost civilization that once thrived in Antarctica, or were they part of a giant cosmic puzzle that transcended human understanding?

The explorers' discoveries raised more questions than answers, plunging them deeper into a labyrinth of uncertainty and intrigue. The Ice Wall, once thought to be a mere natural formation, now loomed before them as a gateway to a realm of limitless possibilities. Each discovery only deepened the mystery of this icy frontier, beckoning the explorers to venture further into its icy depths in search of the truth hidden within its frozen heart.

The Enigmatic Ice Wall

• Shrouded in Ice and Mystery.

Deep within the icy expanse of Antarctica lies a barrier unlike any other on Earth. The Ice Wall, a towering structure of frozen wonder, stretches endlessly in all directions, its secrets locked away from prying eyes. The very sight of this massive ice formation invokes a sense of awe and intrigue, beckoning explorers and researchers to uncover its enigmatic nature.

As the icy wind whispers tales of ancient mysteries, one cannot help but wonder about the origins of this imposing boundary. What forces shaped its formidable presence, and what lies beyond its frozen facade? The answers to these questions remain elusive, buried beneath layers of ice and time.

With its sheer size and imposing beauty, the Ice Wall stands as a silent sentinel at the edge of our known world, challenging our perceptions of reality. Its very existence raises profound questions about our planet's nature and the mysteries hidden within its icy core. As the sun dips below the horizon, casting long shadows across the frozen landscape, the Ice Wall seems to come alive with whispers of forgotten secrets and untold tales.

For centuries, explorers and scholars have been drawn to the icy allure of the Ice Wall, seeking to unravel its mysteries and unlock the secrets that lie beyond. The very essence of this enigmatic boundary seems to pulse with a silent power, beckoning us to venture deeper into its icy embrace. As we journey closer to the Ice Wall, we are filled with anticipation and curiosity, eager to uncover the hidden truths buried beneath layers of ice and time.

In our quest to unveil the unseen boundary, we must be prepared to confront the unknown and embrace the mysteries. The Ice Wall, with its towering presence and frozen beauty, symbolizes the untamed wilderness and the limitless possibilities that await those brave enough to venture into its frigid depths. Only by delving into the heart of this frozen expanse can we hope to uncover the true nature of this enigmatic barrier and shed light on the secrets that have remained hidden for generations.

- Shrouded in Ice and Mystery

Embedded deep within the icy expanse of the Antarctic lies a realm shrouded in enigma and intrigue. The Ice Wall, a towering barrier that separates our known world from the mysteries that lie beyond, stands as a symbol of the unknown, cloaked in an aura of icy mystery.

As one gazes upon its frost-covered surface, a sense of foreboding and fascination intertwines, drawing the curious ever closer to its edge. The howling winds carry whispers of ancient secrets, civilizations long forgotten, and beings beyond our wildest imaginations.

The Ice Wall's sheer magnitude commands respect. It is a silent sentinel guarding the enigmatic realms that lie beyond its frozen facade. Its towering peaks and crevasses bear witness to passaging time, etched with the stories of those who dared to venture into its icy domain.

Legends speak of lost expeditions, explorers consumed by the icy grasp of the Wall, their fates forever entwined with its mysteries. The shifting shadows cast by the relentless sun play tricks on the mind, distorting reality and blurring the line between truth and illusion.

Yet, amidst the chill and the whispers, there lies a sense of ancient wisdom, a knowledge far beyond our own. The Ice Wall, with all its icy splendor, remains a testament to the boundless mysteries of our world, a gateway to realms unseen and untold.

For those who dare to peer beyond the veil of ice and mystery, a journey of discovery awaits, where the boundaries of imagination are stretched and reality merges with the fantastical.

In the hushed whispers of explorers and scientists alike, a theory persists that the Ice Wall is not merely a natural formation but a construct of an advanced civilization that predated our own. Some believe it was built as a barrier to protect the secrets of a lost civilization hidden beyond its icy embrace. In contrast, others speculate it is a gateway to parallel dimensions or alternate realities.

The stories of those who have braved the treacherous terrain surrounding the Ice Wall are as varied as they are unsettling. Tales of strange lights dancing on the horizon, ghostly apparitions haunting the icy expanse, and unexplained disappearances defying all logical explanations have only added to the mystique and allure of this frozen frontier.

Despite the dangers and uncertainties accompanying any expedition to the Ice Wall, the allure of uncovering its secrets remains a siren's call to the bold and the curious. The lure of the unknown, the promise of discovery, and the thrill of unraveling ancient mysteries continue to beckon adventurers and dreamers from far and wide, their fates forever tied to the icy enigma of the formidable Ice Wall.

- Frozen Barriers of Perception

As explorers venture further into the frozen expanse of the Ice Wall, the barriers of perception grow more pronounced, enveloping them in a shroud of mystery and intrigue. The fabric of reality seems to bend and twist in this ethereal realm, where the laws of physics no longer sway, and the boundaries between the tangible and intangible blur into a mesmerizing dance of light and shadow.

Sounds become hushed echoes, reverberating through the icy landscape like whispers of long-forgotten secrets waiting to be unraveled. Colors shift and blend in a mesmerizing display of hues that seem to defy the human eye's limitations, creating an otherworldly tableau that captivates the senses and stirs the soul.

Time takes on a new meaning within the confines of the ice-bound domain, with moments stretching into infinity and the very concept of past, present, and future losing its distinct boundaries. In this place, the linear progression of time gives way to a more fluid and enigmatic rhythm, one that pulses with the beating heart of the ancient mysteries that permeate the icy expanse.

Yet, amidst the disorienting beauty and unearthly allure of the frozen barriers of perception, there lies a profound sense of introspection and self-discovery that transcends the boundaries of the physical world. It is as if the Ice Wall itself is a living entity, a sentient being that peers into the depths of the explorers' souls and beckons them to confront their innermost fears and desires.

For those willing to brave the enigmatic realm beyond the Ice Wall, a profound transformation awaits. It transcends mere physical exploration and delves deep into the realms of the mind and spirit, where the true nature of existence is laid bare and the boundaries of perception are shattered like shards of ice in the wind.

The explorers grapple with existential questions that echo in the icy silence, pondering reality and their place within it. They are confronted with their mortality, fears, and insecurities laid bare in the unforgiving light of the frozen landscape. Some are driven to the brink of madness, their minds fracturing under the weight of the mysteries confronting them.

But some find solace in the enigmatic beauty of the Ice Wall and embrace the challenge of exploring the depths of their consciousness in search of enlightenment. They understand that the barriers of perception are not limitations, but gateways to a deeper understanding of the world and the truths hidden within their hearts.

So, as the explorers press on into the heart of the Ice Wall, they are forever changed by their experiences. They emerge on the other side not as mere travelers but as seekers of knowledge and truth, forever bound by the icy realm that has touched their souls in ways beyond comprehension.

- Unveiling the Unseen Boundary

In the depths of Antarctica, beyond the reach of conventional exploration, lies a barrier that has captivated the imaginations of many. This unseen boundary, known as the Ice Wall, is a formidable obstacle that separates the known world from the mysteries that lie beyond.

Whispers in ancient texts and indigenous folklore describe the Ice Wall as a boundary between realms, a veil that conceals truths and wonders beyond comprehension. Those who have ventured close to its icy expanse report a sense of foreboding and an inexplicable pull toward the unknown.

As researchers and explorers strive to understand this enigmatic barrier, they encounter challenges that defy logic and reason. Technology falters in the face of the Ice Wall's mysteries, leaving unanswered questions lingering in the frigid air.

What lies beyond this unseen boundary? Are there hidden civilizations, ancient secrets, or perhaps otherworldly beings that dwell in the shadow of the Ice Wall? The allure of the unknown beckons bold adventurers to push beyond the limits of what is known and step into the realm of endless possibility.

In the quest to unveil the unseen boundary, one must be prepared to confront the physical obstacles of the icy expanse and the psychological barriers that stand in the way of understanding. The journey to reveal the truths that lie beyond the Ice Wall is not for the faint of heart, but for those driven by curiosity and a thirst for discovery. The rewards may be beyond imagination.

As the veil of the unseen boundary parts, revealing glimpses of what lies beyond, a sense of wonder and awe permeates the soul. Once a symbol of isolation and separation, the Ice Wall becomes a gateway to a realm of infinite possibilities, waiting to be explored and understood by those brave enough to venture into the unknown.

The legends surrounding the Ice Wall date back centuries, with ancient civilizations attributing mystical properties to its icy facade. Some believe that celestial beings live beyond the barrier, watching over the world with a gaze penetrating reality's very fabric.

Whispers of lost civilizations and forgotten knowledge echo through the windswept expanse of Antarctica, hinting at a past shrouded in secrecy and obscured by time. The Ice Wall is a testament to the enigmatic forces that have shaped our world, guarding its mysteries with an icy silence that defies comprehension.

As modern explorers grapple with the challenges posed by the Ice Wall, they are forced to confront the physical dangers of the harsh polar environment and the metaphysical mysteries that shroud the barrier in a veil of uncertainty. Some claim to have glimpsed strange lights dancing at the ice's edge, hinting at a presence that defies rational explanation.

The quest to uncover the secrets of the Ice Wall continues unabated, drawing in a diverse cast of characters from scientists and scholars to thrill-seekers and conspiracy theorists. Everyone brings their perspective and motivation to the table, adding complexity to the already rich tapestry of lore surrounding the mysterious barrier.

As the sun dips below the horizon, casting long shadows across the frozen landscape, the Ice Wall stands as a silent sentinel, watching over the realms of the known and the unknown. What lies beyond its icy facade remains a mystery waiting to be unraveled, beckoning those brave enough to venture into the depths of the Antarctic wilderness in search of truth and discovery.

Mythical Realms Beyond

As the explorers ventured further into the icy wastelands, the ancient whispers grew louder, swirling around them like ghostly mist. With each step, the remnants of a once-great civilization became more apparent as intricate carvings adorned the frozen walls, telling stories of a civilization long forgotten by time.

They discovered a chamber among the ruins unlike any they had seen before. The walls were lined with shimmering crystals that glowed with an ethereal light, casting dancing shadows across the icy floor. In the center of the chamber stood a pedestal, upon which rested a mysterious artifact—a crystal orb pulsating with a faint, otherworldly energy.

Drawn by the orb's mesmerizing glow, one explorer reached out to touch it, and in an instant, a flood of images and memories flooded their minds. They saw visions of a highly advanced society where technology and nature were intricately intertwined and where knowledge was revered above all else.

But as quickly as the visions came, they faded, leaving a haunting sense of loss and longing. The explorers realized they were standing in a place that had once been a sanctuary of wisdom and power, now reduced to ruins buried beneath the ice.

As they continued to explore the chamber, they uncovered more artifacts that hinted at the civilization's mastery over the elements. Tablets inscribed with complex symbols detailed intricate rituals that harnessed the forces of nature, while intricate devices lay dormant, waiting to be awakened by a touch long forgotten.

The explorers felt awe and reverence for the ancient civilization that had come before them, and a deep curiosity stirred within their hearts. What had led to the downfall of such a powerful and enigmatic society? And what secrets lay hidden within the icy depths, waiting to be unearthed by those brave enough to seek them out?

With each discovery, the expedition teams delved deeper into the mysteries of the forgotten lands beyond the Ice Wall, their thirst for knowledge driving them ever onward into the unknown. The whispers of the past grew stronger, guiding their path through the frozen expanse as they sought to unravel the secrets buried beneath the ice.

As they journeyed further into the heart of the icy wilderness, a sense of foreboding grew within them, a feeling that they were on the brink of uncovering truths that had long been hidden from the world. The echoes of the ancient civilization called out to them, beckoning them to explore further, to find the mysteries waiting to be discovered in the shadows of Antarctica's icy wastelands.

- Echoes of Forgotten Lands

The explorer trudged through the snow, the icy wind biting at their exposed skin as they pressed forward into the heart of the frozen expanse. The landscape stretched endlessly before them, a pristine white canvas marred only by the footprints they left in their wake. The whispers of forgotten lands echoed in their ears, urging them to uncover the secrets hidden beneath the icy surface.

As the explorers ventured deeper into the unknown, the icy landscape shifted around them, taking on a surreal quality that defied explanation. Shadows danced at the edges of their vision, flickering in and out of existence like phantoms conjured by the frigid air. Ancient runes glowed faintly in the ice, their intricate patterns hinting at a power long lost to the world.

The explorer's heart quickened with excitement and trepidation as they followed the elusive whispers deeper into the frozen expanse. Each step brought them closer to the heart of the mystery, closer to the source of the ancient power that pulsed beneath the ice like a dormant heartbeat.

As they walked, the explorers' senses were assaulted by a cacophony—the howl of the wind, the creaking of shifting ice, the distant rumble of unseen forces at work. The air seemed to hum with a subtle energy, a vibration that resonated deep within their bones and stirred a primal sense of awe within their souls.

And then, just as the explorer reached the peak of a snow-covered ridge, they saw a vast expanse of ruins spread out before them, half-buried beneath the shifting snowdrifts. Crumbled stone structures jutted out from the icy landscape like the bones of a long-dead giant, their weathered surfaces etched with strange symbols and glyphs that seemed to shimmer in the pale light.

The explorers' hearts raced as they realized the magnitude of their discovery—these ruins were not just a remnant of a forgotten civilization but a gateway to an ancient power that held the key to unlocking the mysteries of the forgotten lands. With trembling hands, they reached out to touch the cold stone, feeling a surge of energy flow through their fingertips like the land was alive.

At that moment, as the echoes of forgotten lands reverberated in their ears and the ancient power thrummed beneath their touch, the explorers knew they had stumbled upon something greater than they could have ever imagined. With a sense of reverence and determination burning in their souls, they set out to delve deeper into the enigma of the frozen expanse, ready to unlock the secrets that lay hidden beneath the icy surface.

- Veiled in Myth and Legend

In the frigid expanse beyond the Ice Wall, whispers of ancient myths and legends echo through the icy winds, shrouding the mysterious boundary in a veil of captivating lore. Stories passed down through generations speak of hidden realms and mythical beings that live beyond the icy barrier, sparking the imagination and fueling the thirst for discovery.

Legends tell of lost civilizations that once thrived in the frozen landscapes, their majestic cities now buried beneath layers of snow and ice. Tales of heroic explorers who braved the treacherous terrain in search of these mythical realms are woven into the fabric of history; their daring adventures are immortalized in epic sagas.

Among the most enduring myths is that of the fabled city of Antarkaya, said to be a romantic paradise hidden deep within the icy heart of Antarctica. It is whispered that the town is inhabited by an ancient and enigmatic race of beings who possess extraordinary powers and knowledge far beyond that of mortal men. Some believe that the inhabitants of Antarkaya are the descendants of a lost civilization that predates recorded history, while others dismiss the legend as pure fantasy.

The veil of myth and legend surrounding the Ice Wall tantalizes and mystifies, drawing intrepid explorers and truth-seekers from far and wide in search of the truth behind the ancient stories. As they journey into the unknown, they face the challenge of separating fact from fiction, navigating the blurred lines between reality and myth that converge at the frozen frontier.

In the shadows of the Ice Wall, whispers of forgotten tales linger, beckoning those who dare to unravel the enigmatic truths that lie beyond. Here, in the realm of myth and legend, the boundaries of imagination and reality blur, inviting the brave and the curious to venture forth and discover the secrets that have long been veiled in mystery.

As explorers venture closer to the Ice Wall, they notice strange phenomena that defy explanation. Whispers of ghostly figures moving among the icy cliffs, ethereal lights dancing on the horizon, and the eerie sensation of being watched from unseen eyes add to the mystery surrounding the boundary. Some claim to have glimpsed shadowy shapes flitting through the blizzard, disappearing as quickly as they appear, leaving only a sense of unease and wonder behind.

Rumors persist of a hidden gateway within the Ice Wall, a portal to another world where time flows differently and reality is a fluid concept. Those who have ventured too close to the boundary speak of strange visions and unexplained phenomena that defy logic, drawing them further into the enigmatic depths of the frozen realm. The boundary between myth and reality blurs as explorers face challenges that test their beliefs and push the limits of their understanding of the world.

The Ice Wall guards untold mysteries, a boundary between the known and the unknown, the real and the imagined. As the whispers of ancient legends echo through the icy winds, beckoning the brave and the curious to explore the secrets that lie beyond, the Ice Wall remains a tantalizing enigma, a testament to the enduring power of myth and mystery in the frozen expanse of the edge of the world.

The allure of the Ice Wall is not merely in its physical presence, but also in the enigmatic energy that seems to emanate from its very core. Some say that the Ice Wall holds within it a reservoir of ancient wisdom and cosmic power, a source of energy that defies conventional scientific explanation. Explorers who have spent time in its vicinity speak of feeling a strange pull towards the wall as if it holds the key to unlocking the mysteries of the universe itself.

Whispers abound of a secret society that has long sought to unravel the secrets of the Ice Wall, delving into ancient texts and esoteric knowledge in their quest for enlightenment. These enigmatic scholars are said to possess knowledge that spans the ages, passed down through generations in a sacred tradition of wisdom and mystery. They are rumored to hold the key to unlocking the secrets of the Ice Wall and revealing the truth behind its enigmatic facade.

As the sun dips below the horizon, casting long shadows across the icy landscape, the whispers of the Ice Wall grow louder, filling the air with a sense of ancient power and untold secrets waiting to be uncovered. The boundary between reality and myth blurs even further as explorers prepare to venture into the heart of the frozen frontier, where the boundaries of time and space seem to converge in a tapestry of enigmatic wonder and mystery.

- Secrets of Ancient Civilizations

In the heart of Antarctica's icy expanse, where the frigid winds moan a haunting melody and the eternal snow blankets the land in a pristine white, a secret remains hidden from the world for millennia. Beneath the frozen surface, nestled within the depths of the enigmatic Ice Wall, lies the remnants of a civilization so ancient that it predates the earliest known histories of humankind.

The pyramids of Antarctica tower majestically above the ice, their angular shapes starkly contrast to the endless white landscape surrounding them. These enigmatic structures, constructed with a precision and symmetry that defies explanation, serve as silent sentinels guarding the secrets of a lost civilization. Each block, expertly carved and placed with meticulous care, whispers of a level of craftsmanship and engineering prowess far beyond what our modern world can comprehend.

As explorers and researchers venture into the heart of Antarctica in search of answers, they are met with challenges that test their resolve and push the boundaries of human knowledge. The ruins hold clues to a society that thrived in this icy wilderness, their artifacts and symbols speaking of a culture steeped in mysticism and cosmic understanding. Hieroglyphs etched into weathered stone tell tales of a people who revered the celestial bodies above, weaving intricate patterns of stars and constellations into their very existence.

Legends speak of a powerful energy source that the ancient Antarcticans harnessed, a force that allowed them to manipulate the very fabric of reality itself. Some whisper of a technology so advanced that it allowed them to traverse vast distances in the blink of an eye, bending space and time to their will. The mysteries of the pyramids and ruins hint at a civilization that transcended the boundaries of our understanding, unlocking secrets of the universe that lay hidden in the shadows of time.

Among the echoes of the past that reverberate through the icy corridors of the Antarctic ruins, a sense of unease lingers, as if the spirits of the ancient Antarcticans watch and wait for those who seek to unravel the enigma of their lost civilization. The secrets buried within the frozen depths hold the key to unlocking a truth that may forever alter our perceptions of history and the cosmos. Only those with the courage to delve deeper into the mysteries beneath the ice and snow will unveil the profound revelations that await within the ancient pyramids of Antarctica.

Shadows of the Unknown

In the depths of the Antarctic, where the icy winds howl and the snow-covered plains stretch endlessly, lies a realm shrouded in mystery and intrigue. Ancient whispers speak of shadowy figures that dwell beyond the icy barrier, beings not of this world but connected to it in ways unfathomable to human understanding.

Stories of encounters with these enigmatic entities have been passed down through generations. Tales of eerie lights dancing in the frigid darkness and strange symbols etched into the icy cliffs have been passed down through generations. Some believe these beings to be extraterrestrial drawn to Earth's frozen frontier for reasons unknown.

Explorers who have ventured close to the ice wall speak of being watched, of unseen eyes following their every move. Some claim to have heard voices on the wind, speaking in languages long forgotten by mortal tongues. These whispers, they say, are the echoes of otherworldly beings communicating across the vast expanse of ice.

But are these shadowy figures indeed alien entities, or are they entirely different? Some theorize that they may be ancient guardians of the Earth, spirits bound to the icy realm to protect its secrets from prying eyes. Others suggest they are interdimensional beings, capable of slipping between the veils of reality and existing simultaneously in multiple planes of existence.

The ice wall itself holds its mysteries. Rumors abound of hidden passages and lost civilizations buried beneath the frozen surface. Some believe the wall is not a natural formation, but a structure built by an ancient and advanced civilization, a barrier erected to protect the world from the eldritch forces that lie beyond.

The truth remains elusive as the Antarctic winds continue to howl and the shadows lengthen in the eternal twilight. Those who seek to uncover the secrets of the ice wall must tread carefully, for the line between reality and myth grows ever thinner in the frozen expanse of Antarctica.

The eerie beauty of the Antarctic landscape belies the hidden dangers that lurk within its icy embrace. As the sun sets on the horizon, casting long shadows across the snow-covered plains, a sense of unease settles over the explorers who dare to venture into this forbidding realm.

Whispers of ancient civilizations lost to time drift on the icy winds, their voices barely audible but laden with a weight of sorrow and longing. Those who have braved the treacherous terrain speak of strange occurrences, inexplicable phenomena that defy rational explanation. It is said that the very fabric of reality bends and warps in the presence of the ice wall as if the laws of nature themselves are but a mere suggestion in this enigmatic domain.

The mystery of the ice wall beckons to those with a thirst for knowledge and a hunger for discovery, drawing them deeper into its icy heart with promises of forgotten secrets and truths waiting to be revealed. But as the shadows deepen and the cold seeps into their bones, they may realize that some mysteries are left untouched, that some truths are better buried beneath the frozen surface.

- Alien Intrigue at the Earth's Edge

As Dr. Isabella Frost continued deciphering the ancient alien hieroglyphs within the hidden cavern beyond the Ice Wall, a sense of unease gnawed at the edges of her consciousness. The pulsating glow of the shimmering crystals cast eerie shadows on the icy walls, creating a surreal atmosphere that seemed to hum with a strange energy.

The glyphs spoke of a time long ago when the stars aligned in ways unknown to modern eyes, and cosmic forces beyond human comprehension guided the evolution of civilizations across the universe. There were mentions of great cataclysms that reshaped entire worlds, of beings of incomprehensible power who strode among the stars, and of a grand design that connected all creation beyond mortal understanding.

However, as Dr. Frost delved deeper into the enigmatic symbols, she uncovered a darker undercurrent beneath the cosmic beauty veneer. The messages hinted at a hidden agenda, a secret purpose behind the alien visitors' interactions with humanity. Whispers of manipulation and control floated within the intricate designs, painting a chilling picture of power beyond reckoning that sought to shape the destiny of Earth and its inhabitants for its unfathomable ends.

The realization struck Dr. Frost like a thunderbolt, sending shivers down her spine as she realized the implications of her discovery. The alien artifacts she had unearthed were not mere relics of a bygone era, but tools of influence, keys to unlocking a cosmic conspiracy that spanned galaxies and eons. The weight of this knowledge pressed down upon her like a suffocating blanket, filling her with a sense of dread and determination in equal measure.

With each passing moment, the shadows seemed to deepen within the cavern, as if the fabric of reality itself was warping under the weight of the truths she was uncovering. Dr. Isabella Frost knew she stood at a crossroads between enlightenment and oblivion, between revealing the cosmic secrets hidden beyond the Ice Wall and unleashing forces that could rend the fabric of existence.

As she raised her trembling hand to touch the nearest glyph, a power surge coursed through her veins, connecting her to a vast tapestry of knowledge and destiny that stretched beyond time and space. In that moment of transcendent clarity, Dr. Frost knew her journey was far from over—it was just beginning.

- Whisperings of Otherworldly Beings

Deep in the frozen expanse beyond the Ice Wall, whispers of otherworldly beings echo through the icy wasteland. Stories of strange encounters with beings not of this world have long been passed down in hushed tones among explorers and researchers brave enough to venture to the edge of civilization.

These mysterious beings, known as the Frostwalkers, are said to be ancient elemental spirits that have existed since dawn. Legends tell of how they were once mortal beings who became infused with the power of the ice and snow, transcending their physical forms to embody the very essence of the frozen wilderness.

The Frostwalkers are said to possess incredible abilities that defy the laws of nature as we know them. They can manipulate ice and snow with a mere thought, shaping the landscape to their will and weaving intricate patterns of frozen beauty that mesmerize all who behold them. Their presence is often heralded by a chill in the air and a profound stillness descending upon the land.

Some believe that the Frostwalkers are the protectors of the Earth, tasked with maintaining the delicate balance of nature and ensuring the survival of all living things. They are said to watch over the planet from their hidden realm beyond the Ice Wall, guiding its inhabitants towards harmony and understanding with the natural world.

However, some fear the Frostwalkers, believing them harbingers of doom and destruction. Whispers of their wrath have chilled the hearts of even the bravest souls, as tales of frozen landscapes and cursed travelers lost to the icy embrace of the Frostwalkers spread throughout the northern lands.

Rumors suggest the Frost walkers communicate in a language of frost and ice, their words forming intricate crystalline patterns that shimmer and dance with the light. Those who have claimed to have glimpsed these ephemeral messages speak of a profound awe and reverence that overcomes them, as if they are witnessing the essence of magic itself.

Scholars and sages have long debated the true nature of the Frostwalkers, delving into ancient texts and forgotten lore in search of answers. Some believe the Frostwalkers are beings from a realm beyond our own, sent to protect the Earth from unseen threats lurking in the shadows. Others speculate they are manifestations of the collective consciousness of the natural world, embodiments of the primal forces that shape the very fabric of existence.

As the whispers of the Frostwalkers continue to weave their enigmatic web of wonder and intrigue, drawing the curious and the daring deeper into the frozen expanse, one thing remains certain: the mysteries of these otherworldly beings are as boundless and timeless as the icy wilderness they call home.

- Unearthly Connections to the Ice Wall

In the frozen expanse beyond the Ice Wall, whispers of unearthly connections linger in the frigid air. Legends and myths speak of ancient beings with celestial origins who once roamed the icy lands, their presence felt in the subtle shifts of the frozen landscape.

Explorers who braved the treacherous journey to the Ice Wall have reported encountering strange phenomena that defy rational explanation. Whispers of ghostly apparitions dancing in the shimmering auroras, ethereal voices carried on the howling winds, and mysterious lights flickering in the darkness have fueled speculation about otherworldly entities inhabiting the icy realm.

Some believe that the Ice Wall acts as a gateway to dimensions beyond our understanding, where beings of cosmic origins cross into our world, leaving traces of their presence scattered amidst the snow and ice. Ancient texts and oral traditions tell of celestial visitors who descended from the heavens to impart ancient wisdom to the inhabitants of Earth, their knowledge woven into the fabric of reality itself.

As the mysteries of the Ice Wall continue to beckon intrepid explorers and truth-seekers alike, the enigmatic connections to unearthly realms remain shrouded in intrigue and speculation. The veil of the unknown flutters on the icy winds, inviting those who dare to unravel the secrets hidden within the frozen expanse beyond the world's edge.

Nestled within the heart of the ancient ice lies a hidden chamber known only to a select few who have glimpsed its ethereal glow. This chamber, rumored to be a portal to realms beyond comprehension, pulses a mesmerizing light that hums with a cosmic resonance. Those who have dared to venture inside speak of visions that transcend time and space, whispers that echo through their minds' corridors, and a profound sense of connection to something greater than themselves.

The chamber walls are adorned with intricate carvings depicting celestial beings descending from the heavens, their outstretched hands offering knowledge and guidance to those seeking enlightenment. Symbols of unknown origin dance across the icy surfaces, shimmering with an otherworldly luminescence that seems to shift and change with the observer's gaze.

Rumors abound of a secret order of scholars and mystics who guard the chamber, dedicating their lives to deciphering the enigmatic messages encrypted within its walls. Those deemed worthy may be granted access to the chamber's most profound mysteries, unlocking truths hidden for eons beneath the ice.

As the celestial mysteries of the Ice Wall continue to beckon, drawing seekers of truth and wisdom into its icy embrace, the whispers of unearthly connections grow stronger. They weave a tapestry of cosmic enigmas waiting to be unraveled by those who dare venture beyond the edge of the world. Transcending mere physical boundaries, the Ice Wall becomes a threshold for the unknown, where the realms of mortal existence intersect with the infinite expanse of the cosmos.

Concealed Truths and Covert Operations

- Uncovering Hidden Expeditions.

The world beyond the Ice Wall is not just a frozen expanse of ice and snow, but a realm of hidden expeditions and covert operations. Throughout history, there have been whispered tales of covert missions to explore mysteries beyond the icy boundary. These expeditions, shrouded in secrecy and mystery, have sought to uncover the truth in Antarctica's frozen depths.

From government-sponsored missions to private ventures funded by shadowy organizations, these covert operations have delved deep into the unknown, risking life and limb in search of answers to age-old questions. What lies beyond the icy veil? Are there ancient civilizations waiting to be discovered, or perhaps otherworldly beings that have made this desolate land their home?

Despite the dangers and uncertainties, these brave explorers have pushed the boundaries of human knowledge, seeking to unravel the enigmas hidden in the icy shadows. Their stories, often obscured by secrecy and misinformation, offer glimpses into a world few have dared to explore.

As the truth behind these covert operations unravels, new questions arise. What truths have been concealed from the world, and for what purpose? Are there forces at play that seek to keep these secrets away from humanity's prying eyes? Only by delving deeper into the mysteries of the Ice Wall can we hope to uncover the hidden truths and secrets that have been hidden from us for so long.

The journey into concealed truths and covert operations is not for the faint of heart, but for those willing to brave the unknown, the possibilities are endless. As we shine a light into the shadows of Antarctica, we may finally unravel the mysteries that lie beyond the Ice Wall and discover the truth hidden from us for centuries.

Beyond the ice are rumors of lost civilizations and ancient technologies buried beneath the frozen landscape. Some believe that Antarctica's secrets could hold the key to unlocking the mysteries of human history and the origins of our species. Others speak of encounters with strange beings, creatures unlike anything seen before, living in the remote corners of the continent.

Whispers of a hidden network of tunnels and underground facilities spread among those who dare to venture into the icy unknown. Some claim that these tunnels lead to other dimensions or are part of a global conspiracy to control the flow of information and power.

The secrecy surrounding these covert operations only adds to the intrigue and danger of exploring the uncharted territories beyond the Ice Wall, with each expedition that sets out into the icy expanse, the line between reality and myth blurs, leaving us to question what lies hidden in the frozen depths of Antarctica and what motivations drive those who seek to uncover its secrets.

- Uncovering Hidden Expeditions

As the explorers pressed on through the unforgiving Antarctic landscape, their breath forming icy clouds in the frigid air, they couldn't shake the feeling that they were treading upon the ground that had been untouched by human feet for millennia. The frozen wasteland's stark beauty stretched before them, a stark reminder of the vastness of the unknown that lay beyond the Ice Wall.

The expedition leader, a man of few words but infinite wisdom, gazed out across the icy expanse with fierce determination. His mind was a labyrinth of ancient knowledge and forgotten lore, a repository of secrets passed down through generations of explorers who had dared to venture into the depths of the Antarctic wilderness.

As they journeyed more profoundly into the heart of the frozen continent, the explorers encountered strange markings etched into the ice, symbols that seemed to pulse with otherworldly energy. They studied these enigmatic glyphs, feeling a primal sense of unease as they realized they were standing on the threshold of powers far beyond their comprehension.

Whispers of a lost civilization, a race of beings who had once called the frozen wastes of Antarctica their home, haunted the explorers' every step. They could almost sense these ancient beings lurking in the shadows, watching their progress with eyes that gleamed, knowing that transcended time itself.

And then, as they reached the very edge of the Ice Wall, a sense of foreboding settled over the group like a heavy shroud. The leader raised a hand to signal for silence, his eyes scanning the horizon for any sign of movement. An icy wind stirred the surrounding ice, carrying a sense of ancient power that sent shivers down their spines.

At that moment, as the explorers stood on the brink of the unknown, they knew they were about to embark on a journey that would push the boundaries of their understanding to the very limits. The Ice Wall loomed before them like a gateway to a realm of unimaginable wonders and terrors, a barrier that held the key to secrets that had been hidden from the eyes of humanity for untold eons.

With a last glance at each other, the explorers steeled themselves for what lay ahead and took their first tentative steps across the threshold of the Ice Wall into a world where reality blurred with myth and mysteries awaited at every turn. And so, their secret expedition continued, driven by a thirst for knowledge that burned like a flame in the icy heart of the Antarctic wilderness, leading them deeper into the unknown with each passing moment.

- Shadows of Deception in the Ice

As the sun dipped below the horizon, casting long shadows across the icy expanse of Antarctica, a sense of foreboding settled over the isolated research station. Dr. Marlowe, a renowned glaciologist known for his groundbreaking discoveries, felt a gnawing unease in the pit of his stomach as he pored over his latest data.

The recent seismic activity detected deep beneath the frozen surface raised troubling questions that lingered in the air like a tangible presence. Could it be mere geological shifts, or was something more insidious at play? Dr. Marlowe's thoughts raced as he considered the implications of what lay hidden beneath the impenetrable ice.

Whispers of a shadowy organization operating in the region had reached Dr. Marlowe's ears; their motives were unclear, but their presence was undeniable. Rumors swirled among the researchers: tales of missing equipment, unexplained disappearances, and odd occurrences that defied rational explanation.

As Dr. Marlowe delved deeper into his research, a sense of urgency gripped him, driving him to uncover the truth buried beneath Antarctica's icy facade. The harsh landscape seemed to hold its secrets close, resisting all attempts to unravel the mysteries hidden within its frigid heart.

In the dead of night, as the winds howled outside the station and the ice groaned under the weight of ancient history, Dr. Marlowe changed the course of his research forever. Determined to confront the shadows that lurked in the frozen depths, he set out alone into the icy wilderness, his breath misting in the frigid air.

With each step, his sense of unease deepened, and an icy dread settled over him as he ventured further into the unknown. The ice stretched endlessly before him, a vast and desolate landscape that seemed to hold both answers and danger equally.

As Dr. Marlowe's footsteps echoed in the silent expanse, he knew he was drawing closer to the truth, to the heart of the deception that had plagued the researchers and explorers in this unforgiving land. As he pressed on, the shadows danced around him, whispering of secrets long buried and dangers yet to come, a lone figure in a world of ice and lies.

- Government Secrets Beyond the Wall

As the tangled web of government secrets unravels beyond the Ice Wall, a closer examination reveals a complex and interconnected network of covert operations that spans the frozen wastelands of the Earth's edge. Deep within the shadows of secrecy, powerful forces at play engage in a delicate dance of power and manipulation, shaping the course of history in ways unseen by the ordinary citizen.

Revealed through a patchwork of declassified files, eyewitness testimonies, and whistleblowers' accounts, the true extent of government activities beyond the Ice Wall comes to light. From covert research facilities conducting experiments on the fringes of science to black operations seeking to control ancient knowledge hidden in the icy depths, many agendas converge in this remote and forbidding landscape.

Beneath the facade of stability and order promoted by official channels lies a world of intrigue and danger, where rival factions vie for control over the secrets beyond the Wall. Whether pursuing advanced technology, manipulating global events, or preserving long-buried truths, the stakes are high, and the consequences are far-reaching.

As questions mount and the veil of secrecy lifts, a new chapter in the saga of government secrets beyond the Ice Wall emerges. The ethical dilemmas and moral difficulties faced by those entangled in this web of intrigue become ever more pronounced, prompting readers to probe deeper into the complexities of power and authority that shape our world.

In this extended chapter, the elusive truth hidden beyond the Ice Wall beckons, casting a long shadow over the landscape of government secrets and inviting readers to delve deeper into the mysteries that lie beyond reach.

Further exploration reveals a disturbing pattern of manipulation and control exerted by a shadowy cabal that operates with impunity beyond the boundaries of public scrutiny. Whispers of hidden agendas and ulterior motives permeate the corridors of power as individuals navigate a treacherous landscape fraught with deception and betrayal.

Within this labyrinth of clandestine operations, a select few hold the keys to long-buried secrets that could reshape society's very foundations. Ancient prophecies, forgotten technologies, and otherworldly artifacts lie dormant in the frozen expanses beyond the Ice Wall, waiting to be unearthed by those bold enough to seek them out.

As the lines between truth and fiction blur, the quest for knowledge takes on a new urgency, driving individuals to confront their beliefs and allegiances in the face of overwhelming evidence. What lies beyond the Ice Wall may hold the key to unlocking humanity's greatest mysteries–or sealing its fate in darkness forever.

Unraveling the Ice's Mysteries

As explorers braved the treacherous landscapes of Antarctica, they encountered a myriad of scientific enigmas that confounded even the most seasoned researchers. Beneath the continent's icy surface lay a world shrouded in mystery, where ancient secrets whispered through the frozen winds and tantalizing clues beckoned those brave enough to seek answers.

One of the most intriguing mysteries that captivated scientists was discovering microbial life thriving in the harshest conditions imaginable. Locked in a delicate dance of survival, these resilient organisms had adapted to Antarctica's extreme cold and isolation, challenging the very definition of life itself. How had these microscopic wonders endured for centuries, hidden in the icy depths, defying the harsh realities of their frozen realm?

As researchers delved deeper into Antarctica's heart, they uncovered a puzzle of geological proportions etched into the very fabric of the ice. Remnants of ancient tectonic movements and long-lost continents lay beneath the frozen surface, their silent whispers telling tales of a long-forgotten world. The gradual dance of ice and rock revealed a history of upheaval and transformation, painting a portrait of a continent in constant flux.

The enigmatic magnetic anomalies that permeated the region continued to confound scientists, hinting at forces beyond the scope of conventional understanding. Could these mysterious signals be remnants of a bygone era when Earth's magnetic field held sway over the icy expanse? Or were they harbingers of something more profound, a tantalizing glimpse into the hidden depths of Antarctica's secrets?

As the quest to unravel these mysteries progressed, researchers grappled with profound questions that extended far beyond the continent's icy confines. Each discovery opened new avenues of inquiry, challenging established paradigms and beckoning explorers to venture deeper into the unknown. The enigmas of Antarctica were not just scientific puzzles to be solved, but gateways to a deeper understanding of our world and our place within it.

The quest for knowledge continued unabated in the icy heart of Antarctica, where time stood still, and the winds carried echoes of ancient whispers. The continent held within its frozen grasp the keys to unlocking secrets that had long evaded human comprehension, promising a journey of discovery that would forever alter our perception of the enigmatic realm at the world's edge.

As the sun dipped below the horizon, casting a soft glow over the frozen expanse, a sense of awe and wonder enveloped the intrepid explorers. They realized Antarctica was not just a remote land of ice and snow but a place of profound mystery and intrigue, where the very fabric of reality seemed to shimmer with hidden truths waiting to be revealed. And so, they pressed forward, their hearts ablaze with the promise of discovery and the thrill of uncovering the enigmas buried in the icy depths of Antarctica's timeless embrace.

- Scientific Enigmas of Antarctica

Scientists have long been captivated by the mysteries hidden beneath Antarctica's vast icy surface. The continent's extreme conditions and remote location make it a challenging yet fascinating environment for researchers to explore.

One of Antarctica's scientific enigmas is the discovery of ancient ice cores that provide invaluable insights into Earth's past climate. These ice cores, extracted from deep within Antarctica's ice sheets, contain a record of atmospheric gases, temperature variations, and even traces of ancient organisms. By analyzing these ice cores' chemical composition and physical properties, scientists can reconstruct the history of the planet's climate over hundreds of thousands of years.

Researchers have documented past periods of rapid climate change by studying ice cores, such as abrupt warming events and atmospheric carbon dioxide level shifts. These findings contribute to our understanding of natural climate variability and provide an essential context for assessing the impacts of human-induced climate change.

Antarctica is also home to unique ecosystems adapted to survive in the continent's harsh conditions. From microscopic algae living in the ice to penguins braving the frigid waters, an array of organisms call Antarctica home. Scientists study these ecosystems to uncover the strategies that enable life to thrive in such extreme environments and to investigate the interconnected relationships between species in this remote corner of the world.

The continent's colossal ice sheets regulate global sea levels and ocean circulation patterns. As climate change speeds up Antarctica's ice melt, scientists are working to understand the potential repercussions for coastal communities worldwide. Research efforts focus on predicting the future rate of ice loss, evaluating the stability of ice shelves, and assessing the feedback loops that could amplify the effects of melting ice on the global climate system.

In their quest to unlock Antarctica's scientific enigmas, researchers push the boundaries of knowledge and technology, braving the cold and isolation to uncover the secrets hidden within this icy realm. Their work expands our understanding of the planet and inspires awe and wonder at the marvels of the natural world.

Beyond scientific endeavors, Antarctica holds a unique cultural significance. It is a continent that has captured the imagination of explorers, artists, and writers throughout history. The tales of early Antarctic expeditions, from Shackleton's heroic efforts to Scott's groundbreaking research, have become legendary stories of human resilience and determination in the face of extreme adversity.

Moreover, Antarctica serves as a global laboratory for international cooperation and diplomacy. The Antarctic Treaty, signed in 1959, established the continent as a place of peace and scientific collaboration, setting aside political differences in favor of shared research and environmental protection goals. Today, countries worldwide work together to address the challenges of climate change, environmental conservation, and sustainable resource management in Antarctica.

As we contemplate Antarctica's vast mysteries, we are reminded of our planet's interconnectedness and the urgent need to safeguard its fragile ecosystems for future generations. Through continued scientific exploration and international cooperation, we can unlock the secrets of this icy continent and ensure its protection for years to come.

- Icy Riddles and Climate Conundrums

In the heart of Antarctica, where the chilly winds howl and the ice stretches endlessly towards the horizon, lies a mystery as old as time. The Ice Wall, a towering barricade of frost and secrecy, holds within its frozen grasp enigmas that have puzzled scientists and explorers for centuries.

With each step closer to the icy barrier, the air grows colder, the sky darker, and the whispers of the unknown become louder. Here, on the cusp of the Ice Wall, the boundaries of reality blur, and the line between fact and fiction becomes indistinguishable.

Among the frozen expanse, riddles and mysteries are waiting to be unraveled. From the shifting patterns of the ice to the elusive currents of the Southern Ocean, each aspect of this frigid realm holds its enigma, its puzzle to be deciphered.

But not just the icy landscape challenges those who dare to venture beyond the veil. The harsh and unforgiving climate itself poses its own set of conundrums. The delicate balance of the Earth's systems, intricately linked to the frozen continent, shifts and sways in ways that defy comprehension.

As the sun dips below the horizon, casting long shadows over the icy terrain, the true extent of the mysteries surrounding the Ice Wall becomes clear. What forces lie at play in this desolate landscape? What secrets are buried beneath the frozen surface, waiting to be laid bare?

It is amid these icy riddles and climate problems that the true nature of the Ice Wall reveals itself. As the cold seeps into the bones of those brave enough to seek the truth, one thing becomes abundantly clear—the mysteries of Antarctica are as vast and deep as the ice that covers its ancient secrets.

Beyond the confines of the Ice Wall, a world shrouded in mystery and intrigue beckons to those willing to brave its treacherous depths. Strange phenomena, from unexplained weather patterns to anomalous seismic activity, defy all conventional understanding and push the limits of human knowledge to the brink.

Whispers of ancient civilizations and lost technologies echo through the icy wasteland, hinting at a history far more complex and enigmatic than previously imagined. Some believe the Ice Wall is the key to unlocking these secrets, a gateway to realms beyond our wildest imaginations.

As the icy winds howl with an otherworldly fury and the barren landscape stretches out into infinity, the true extent of the mysteries lurking within Antarctica's icy heart becomes all too clear. The Ice Wall stands as a sentinel, guarding the secrets of the frozen continent with an unyielding resolve that challenges all who dare to venture into its icy embrace.

In the shadows of the Ice Wall, whispers of an ancient civilization that predates human history grow louder, hinting at a lost world buried beneath the ice. Legends speak of a technologically advanced society that harnessed the power of the elements, wielding forces beyond comprehension.

As explorers delve deeper into the frozen expanse, uncovering relics of a long-forgotten time, the truth behind these whispered tales takes shape. Structures of unknown origin emerge from the ice, their purpose and function a mystery waiting to be unraveled.

But with each revelation comes a new enigma, a new puzzle to solve. The very nature of reality itself seems to warp and shift within the confines of the Ice Wall, challenging the perceptions and beliefs of those who dare to explore its depths.

And as the icy winds carry echoes of a forgotten past and a future unknown, the genuine mystery of the Ice Wall becomes clearer than ever. Beneath the frozen surface lies a world of wonders and terrors, secrets and revelations, waiting to be discovered by those brave enough to seek the truth.

The Ice Wall stands as a testament to humankind's resilience and curiosity, a symbol of our insatiable thirst for knowledge and understanding. As the icy barriers that separate us from the unknown crumble, a new chapter in the saga of Antarctica's mysteries unfolds, beckoning to all who dare to venture beyond the confines of the Ice Wall.

- Challenging the Ice Wall's Illusions

In the frigid expanse of the polar regions lies a formidable natural wonder that has captured the imagination of adventurers and scholars alike - the Ice Wall. Towering and imposing, this icy barrier stretches across vast expanses of land, its sheer magnitude sparking curiosity and awe in equal measure.

As we venture deeper into the mysteries of the Ice Wall, we are confronted with many questions and contemplations. What forces sculpted this colossal formation into existence, and what secrets lay buried within its frozen confines? Geological processes that span millennia have shaped the Ice Wall into a formidable structure, revealing layers of history etched into its very core.

Explorers and researchers have long sought to unravel the enigmas of the Ice Wall, embarking on dangerous expeditions to uncover its hidden truths. Yet, the veil of secrecy that shrouds this icy citadel remains impenetrable, with whispers of ancient civilizations and lost knowledge echoing through the frigid winds.

As we navigate the complexities of the Ice Wall, we are compelled to challenge our perceptions and assumptions about this icy frontier. Are the illusions that dance upon its surface mere tricks of light and shadow, or do they hint at more profound layers of reality that elude our understanding? The interplay of light and ice creates a shifting canvas of illusions, inviting us to peer beyond the surface and into the heart of this frozen monolith.

In our quest to unravel the mysteries of the Ice Wall, we are urged to confront the limits of human knowledge and imagination. What undiscovered wonders and terrors lurk within its icy embrace, waiting to be unearthed by intrepid explorers and daring adventurers? The Ice Wall stands as a testament to the enduring allure of the unknown, beckoning us to probe its mysteries and challenge the very fabric of our reality.

As we delve deeper into the lore surrounding the Ice Wall, legends emerge of ancient civilizations that once thrived in the shadow of its icy expanse. Whispers of lost technologies and forgotten wisdom permeate the frigid winds, hinting when the Ice Wall was not merely a natural wonder but a gateway to realms beyond our understanding.

The shifting hues of the Ice Wall, ranging from ethereal blues to stark whites, tell a tale of constant change and transformation. Each crack and crevice in its surface holds a story untold, a history waiting to be revealed to those who dare to venture into its icy realm. The very essence of the Ice Wall seems to pulse with hidden energy, a primal force that tugs at the strings of our curiosity and beckons us to explore its depths.

As we stand at the foot of the Ice Wall, humbled by its sheer magnificence, we are reminded of the vast mysteries that lie beyond the boundaries of our knowledge. The Ice Wall stands as a testament to the enduring mysteries of our world, a reminder that there are still realms to be discovered and truths to be uncovered. And so, we continue to gaze upon the icy expanse, ever drawn to the untold secrets hidden within its frozen embrace.

Chronicles from the Frigid Frontier

As the explorers ventured further into the frozen labyrinth of the Ice Wall, a sense of unreality enveloped them like a heavy shroud. The air seemed to vibrate with ethereal energy, sending tingles of anticipation down their spines and sparking a deep-seated curiosity that drove them onward despite the eerie whispers that echoed through the icy corridors.

The surrounding walls took on a surreal quality, their crystalline surfaces refracting the dim light in kaleidoscopic patterns that danced and shifted with every step. Shadows flickered and danced on the icy floor, hinting at hidden passageways and secret chambers just out of reach. The explorers felt like they had entered a surreal dreamscape, where reality and fantasy intermingled in a dizzying blur of shapes and colors.

In the depths of the Ice Wall, they stumbled upon ancient runes etched into the icy walls. Their meanings were lost to time but resonated with a deep, primal power that stirred something long dormant within them. The glyphs seemed to pulse with a faint, inner light, as if imbued with hidden wisdom that beckoned the explorers to decipher their cryptic messages and unlock the secrets they held.

As they pressed on, drawn inexorably towards the heart of the Ice Wall, they encountered strange geometric formations that defied all logic and reason. Crystalline structures spiraled upwards like frozen tornadoes, casting intricate patterns of light and shadow that seemed to shift and warp with each passing moment. The explorers felt a sense of awe and wonder wash over them, mingled with a creeping unease at the alien beauty surrounding them.

Finally, they reached the central chamber, a vast cavern of shimmering ice that pulsed with a palpable energy that set their hearts racing. The towering monolith of black ice stood in the center of the chamber, its surface marked with a mesmerizing array of symbols and sigils that seemed to writhe and twist in an unseen breeze. The explorers approached with a mixture of trepidation and wonder, knowing they stood on the threshold of something truly extraordinary.

As they reached out to touch the monolith, a power surge coursed through their bodies, connecting them to a vast, unseen energy network that spanned the cosmos. Visions flooded their minds, fragments of forgotten lore and ancient truths that shimmered like mirages on the edge of consciousness. At that moment, they realized that the Ice Wall was not merely a physical barrier, but a gateway to a realm of infinite possibility and boundless discovery—an invitation to explore the fabric of existence itself.

- Frozen Tales of Exploration

In the frigid expanse beyond the Ice Wall, tales of exploration weave a tapestry of mystery and wonder. Brave adventurers venture into the icy unknown, facing frostbite and peril as they push the boundaries of human knowledge. From the creaking ice shelves to the rugged peaks of hidden mountains, each expedition uncovers new wonders and challenges. The howling winds whisper secrets of the ancient ice, guiding intrepid explorers into realms where time stands still. These frozen tales of exploration are etched in the annals of history, a testament to humanity's unyielding spirit of discovery in the face of nature's icy embrace.

As explorers delve deeper into the frozen wilderness, they encounter the physical challenges of the harsh environment and the haunting remnants of past civilizations that once thrived in these snow-covered lands. Ancient ruins, half-buried beneath layers of ice and snow, offer tantalizing glimpses into a bygone era when the frozen landscape teemed with life and activity. Mysterious symbols etched into icy walls hint at a forgotten language, while ornate carvings on icy pillars depict scenes of a lost civilization's daily life.

The explorers press on, guided by their insatiable curiosity and the allure of undiscovered treasures hidden in the icy depths. They brave treacherous crevasses and unpredictable blizzards, their footsteps echoing in the empty vastness of the frozen realm. The howling winds carry whispers of long-forgotten stories of ancient kings and queens who once ruled over this frozen domain with an iron fist.

As they journey into the icy unknown, the explorers unravel the secrets of the Ice Wall, piecing together a mosaic of history and myth that sheds light on the enigmatic world beyond. Each discovery brings them closer to the heart of the frozen wilderness, where ancient truths lie waiting to be uncovered by those bold enough to seek them out. And so, the saga of exploration continues, weaving a tale of courage, discovery, and the limitless boundaries of human imagination in the face of nature's icy embrace.

As the explorers venture deeper into the frozen wilderness, they notice subtle changes in the landscape. Strange rock formations jut out from the ice, their surfaces adorned with intricate carvings telling stories of a long-forgotten civilization. The explorers painstakingly document each carving, trying to decipher the cryptic messages left behind by those who once called this icy realm home.

The howling winds seem to carry voices from the past, haunting whispers that stir the explorers' souls with a sense of foreboding. Yet, they press on, driven by a relentless thirst for knowledge and a desire to unlock the mysteries of the frozen wilderness. As they climb higher into the mountains, the air grows thinner, and each step becomes a test of endurance and determination.

Finally, after days of grueling trekking, the explorers reach a massive structure that looms ominously in the distance. Half-buried in the ice, the structure radiates an aura of ancient power and majesty. As they draw closer, they realize it is a temple, its icy walls adorned with symbols of a civilization long lost to time.

With trembling hands, they push open the massive doors of the temple, revealing a vast chamber filled with treasures beyond imagination. Golden artifacts glint in the dim light, their surfaces covered in intricate patterns and symbols of a glorious past. The explorers stand in awe, realizing they have stumbled upon a treasure trove of unparalleled historical significance.

But as they marvel at the riches before them, a deep rumbling shakes the temple walls, sending ice and snow cascading around them. The explorers realize they have awakened a slumbering guardian, a creature of ice and fury that has remained dormant for centuries. With hearts pounding, they know they must escape with their lives and the knowledge they have gained before the guardian unleashes its frozen wrath upon them.

And so, the explorers flee from the temple, their minds reeling with the wonders and terrors they have encountered in the frozen wilderness. Yet, even as they race back towards the safety of their camp, they know that the mysteries of the icy realm will continue to beckon, drawing them ever deeper into the enigmatic heart of the Ice Wall.

- Descending into the Unknown

The explorers stood at the foot of the towering Ice Wall, their breath visible in the frigid air as they marveled at the sheer magnitude of the icy barrier before them. The sun dipped lower on the horizon, casting long shadows that danced across the frozen landscape, adding to the otherworldly mystery that enveloped the area.

As they gazed upward, the intricate patterns and formations of the ice came into sharper focus, revealing a tapestry of frozen beauty that seemed to pulse with a life of its own. It was as if the Ice Wall held within its depths a story waiting to be unraveled, a history that begged to be discovered.

One explorer, a seasoned mountaineer with a gleam of excitement in his eyes, raised his hand to shield his face from the sun's blinding reflection off the ice. He could sense the allure of the unknown pulling at him, beckoning him to delve deeper into the mysteries hidden within the icy expanse.

With a shared nod of determination, the group began their ascent, carefully picking their way through the treacherous terrain as they made their way closer to the towering columns of ice that loomed above them. The air grew colder, the silence more profound, amplifying the sense of isolation and solitude that permeated the landscape.

They moved with cautious determination, their hearts pounding in rhythm with the crunch of their boots on the frozen ground. Shadows danced at the edges of their vision, elusive and ethereal, as if the spirits of those who had come before guided them on their journey into the unknown.

As they ventured further into the heart of the Ice Wall, the surrounding structures grew more intricate and awe-inspiring. Spiraling towers of ice rose majestically into the sky, their surfaces adorned with delicate patterns and carvings that spoke of craftsmanship far beyond their comprehension.

The explorers felt a sense of reverence wash over them, a deep understanding that they were standing on the threshold of something truly extraordinary. The ice seemed to hum with an energy all its own, resonating with a power that pulsed through the very core of their beings.

With each step they took, the explorers felt drawn further into the enigmatic world of the Ice Wall, where time seemed to stand still, and reality bent to the will of ancient forces. They knew they were on the brink of uncovering truths that would forever change their understanding of the world and their place within it. And so, with a mixture of trepidation and exhilaration, they pressed on, ready to plunge deeper into the icy embrace of the unknown.

- Journals of Ice Wall Voyagers

In the frozen expanse beyond the Ice Wall, tales of daring voyagers who braved the icy depths in search of truth and adventure exist. Their journals, weathered by time and frost, vividly depict the challenges and wonders they encountered in this mysterious realm.

As the explorers ventured into the unknown, their entries spoke of the haunting beauty of the icy landscape, where towering glaciers glistened in the pale sunlight and ancient rock formations held secrets of a bygone era. They described the eerie silence that enveloped them, broken only by the occasional howl of the icy winds that whipped across the barren wasteland.

Despite the harsh conditions, these courageous individuals pressed on, driven by an insatiable curiosity and a determination to unlock the secrets hidden within the icy fortress. Their accounts detailed encounters with strange creatures, glimpses of long-forgotten ruins, and the unshakeable feeling that they were treading on the edge of reality itself.

With each page turn, readers were transported into a world where time stood. Still, the rules of nature seemed to bend and twist, and the line between dream and reality blurred into a surreal tapestry of ice and shadows. The journals of these intrepid voyagers stood as a testament to the human spirit's thirst for discovery and its unyielding quest for the unknown.

Through their words, we glimpse the enigmatic Ice Wall's allure, beckoning those bold enough to seek its mysteries and unravel the secrets beyond its frozen facade.

In the shadows of the towering ice cliffs, legends whispered of an ancient civilization that once thrived in these icy realms. Their advanced technology and knowledge of the cosmos are now lost in the swirling mists of time. The explorers uncovered ruins that hinted at a once-great society, their intricate carvings and mysterious symbols sparking a deep sense of wonder and intrigue.

As they delved deeper into the icy wilderness, the very fabric of reality seemed to shift and warp around them, casting doubts about what was real and what was a figment of their imagination. Strange lights danced in the sky, casting an ethereal glow over the frozen landscape, while whispers of long-forgotten voices echoed on the icy winds, luring the adventurers further into the heart of the unknown.

Each step they took brought them closer to the truth buried beneath the layers of ice and snow, a truth that promised to unravel the mysteries of the Ice Wall and perhaps even the universe itself. And so, with hearts ablaze and minds alight with curiosity, they pressed onward, driven to unlock the secrets hidden for eons in the frozen expanse beyond the Ice Wall.

As they ventured deeper into the icy realm, the boundaries of space and time seemed to merge and meld, creating a surreal landscape where reality and imagination intertwined in a breathtaking dance. The explorers encountered phenomena that defied all logic and reason, from shimmering auroras that danced across the sky to strange mirages that led them astray.

Amidst the icy expanse, they stumbled upon ancient artifacts that spoke of a civilization long forgotten, their intricate designs hinting at a level of sophistication beyond their wildest dreams. The explorers delved into the mysteries of these relics, piecing together fragments of a lost history that revealed a rich tapestry of culture and knowledge that once thrived in this icy wasteland.

But as they journeyed further into the heart of the Ice Wall, they sensed a presence watching them from the shadows, a primal force that seemed to stir the very essence of their souls. Whispers of ancient legends spoke of a guardian that protected the secrets of the Ice Wall, a being of boundless power and unfathomable wisdom.

With each passing day, the explorers felt the weight of the guardian's gaze upon them, a silent warning that they were treading on sacred ground where mortals were not meant to wander. Yet their thirst for knowledge and discovery drove them ever forward, deeper into the icy labyrinth that held the key to unlocking the mysteries of the universe.

As they stood on the precipice of truth and transformation, the explorers knew that the path ahead would test not only their courage and resolve but also their very understanding of reality. For beyond the shimmering veil of ice and snow lay a realm of wonders and terrors, where the past and present merged in an eternal dance of shadow and light, beckoning forth those brave enough to embrace the unknown and unlock the secrets that lay buried within the frozen expanse beyond the Ice Wall.

Life's Unseen Domain

As explorers continued their journey into the uncharted territories beyond the ice wall, the mysteries of alien ecosystems unfolded in all their complex glory. Each step on the frozen ground revealed an additional layer of diversity and adaptation that defied the imagination. From microscopic organisms thriving in the icy depths to massive predators lurking in the shadows, the richness of life beyond the barrier was a testament to nature's incredible resilience.

Researchers delved deeper into the enigmatic realm and uncovered evidence of ancient civilizations that once ruled these frozen lands. Crumbling structures veiled in ice and snow hinted at sophistication and ingenuity far beyond anything known in the modern world. Artifacts buried in the permafrost told tales of a society steeped in mysticism and knowledge, their purpose and origins shrouded in the mists of time.

The flora and fauna that inhabited the unseen domain were like nothing seen before, their adaptations pushing the boundaries of what was thought possible. Bioluminescent plants danced in the dark, their ethereal glow casting a spectral light on the frozen landscape. Creatures with intricate patterns and colors adorned their bodies, camouflaging themselves against the icy backdrop with a mastery that spoke of evolution's extended hand.

Deeper into this alien world, the explorers encountered phenomena that defied all known scientific principles. Geysers of steaming water erupted from the ice, hinting at a hidden warmth beneath the frozen surface. Crystalline formations, glowing with an inner light, sparkled like jewels in the eternal twilight. The air seemed to hum with a strange energy, as if the land was alive with a consciousness beyond human comprehension.

As the explorers ventured further into this realm of wonders, they felt a profound connection to the forces of nature that shaped this hidden world. It was where time seemed to stand still, where the ancient and the modern collided in a symphony of existence. As they continued their journey, each discovery and revelation only deepened their respect for Earth's last frontier's vast and awe-inspiring complexity.

- Alien Ecosystems Beyond the Barrier

As explorers ventured deeper into the enigmatic realm beyond the Ice Wall, a sense of awe and trepidation enveloped them. The alien ecosystems they encountered seemed to pulsate with primal energy, an ancient force that defied comprehension. In the frigid depths, where sunlight rarely reached, bioluminescent fungi carpeted the floors of vast caverns, their gentle glow casting eerie shadows on towering ice formations that seemed to defy gravity.

The flora that clung to the icicle-laden rocks displayed a bewildering array of colors and shapes, some emitting a faint hum that resonated with the explorers' very bones. Fragile tendrils of iridescent plants brushed against their skin, leaving a tingling sensation that spoke of a connection to forces beyond human understanding.

The creatures that inhabited this frozen domain were like nothing seen before, their adaptations to the extreme cold and darkness a testament to the relentless drive of life to survive. Sleek and curved beings darted through icy waters, their translucent bodies shimmering with an inner light that mesmerized the onlookers. Strange cries echoed through the underground tunnels, reverberating off walls of ice that seemed to hum in response, as if the very rocks possessed a consciousness of their own.

As the explorers delved deeper into the heart of this alien world, they could feel a change in the air, a subtle shift in the fabric of reality that blurred the boundaries between what was known and what was yet to be discovered. Whispers of long-forgotten myths and legends danced on the icy breeze, stirring memories of a time when the Earth itself was but a primordial soup of chaos and creation.

In this realm beyond the Ice Wall, the explorers stood on the threshold of something greater than themselves, a mystery so profound that it defied description. Here, amid the frozen wonders of a world hidden from human eyes, they glimpsed the universe's vastness and the infinite possibilities that lay just beyond the edge of their understanding.

Beyond the shimmering walls of ice, a labyrinthine network of tunnels stretched into the unknown, beckoning the explorers further into the depths of the underground world. The air grew colder, carrying the scent of ancient mysteries long forgotten by time. Strange symbols etched into the ice-covered walls seemed to pulse with a faint, otherworldly light, whispering secrets of a forgotten civilization that once thrived in this icy realm.

As they navigated through the twisting passageways, the explorers encountered strange artifacts of unknown origin, their intricate designs hinting at a level of technology far beyond anything seen in the world above. Tools made of a shimmering, metallic substance lay scattered about, their purpose and function a mystery that tormented the minds of the explorers. It was as if they had stumbled upon a lost city buried deep beneath the ice, a remnant of a civilization that had perished eons ago, leaving only enigmatic traces of its existence.

Amidst the ruins, a deep sense of unease crept into the hearts of the explorers, a primal instinct warning them of the ancient powers that slumbered beneath the frozen surface. Whispers of a forgotten prophecy echoed through the ice, foretelling a great cataclysm that would shake the foundations of the world and unleash forces beyond human comprehension. And as they gazed into the depths of that icy abyss, they knew they stood at the precipice of a revelation that would forever alter their perception of reality.

- Mysteries of Otherworldly Civilizations

In the depths beyond the Ice Wall, where the bitter cold seeps into the bones of even the bravest explorers, whispers the echo of ancient civilizations that exist beyond the realm of human comprehension. Shrouded in mystery and cloaked in enigmatic power, these beings are said to wield knowledge and abilities far beyond anything known to mortals.

Legends tell of a race of cosmic beings who transcend the boundaries of time and space, existing in dimensions beyond our understanding. Known as the Elders of the Void, they are said to be the architects of the universe, shaping reality with a subtlety and finesse that belies their immense power. Whispers of their existence have persisted for eons, passed down through generations in hushed tones of reverence and fear.

The Elders are said to dwell in the furthest reaches of the cosmos, beyond the reach of mortal minds. Their motives and intentions are mysterious, their actions guided by an ancient wisdom that defies human comprehension. Some believe they watch over the universe, guiding its evolution benevolently. In contrast, others fear their influence, warning of the dangers of seeking to unravel the mysteries of their existence.

Yet, despite the warnings, a select few have dared to venture into the unknown, seeking to uncover the truth about the Elders and their enigmatic civilization. Tales of encounters with these cosmic beings are rare and shrouded in ambiguity, with those who return speaking in cryptic riddles and half-truths. Artifacts rumored to be of Elder origin have been discovered on distant worlds, their purpose and significance a mystery that continues to confound even the most brilliant minds.

As the whispers of the Elders persist, pulling at the threads of curiosity and wonder, the allure of the unknown beckons. For those who dare to seek the truth, the journey into the depths beyond the Ice Wall promises untold revelations, as the secrets of the cosmic beings who dwell in realms beyond our understanding await discovery.

Venturing further into the cosmic mysteries, some scholars believe that the Elders of the Void are not bound by the constraints of time as we know it. They exist in a perpetual state of being, able to observe the ebb and flow of the universe from a vantage point that transcends the linear progression of mortal lives. Their influence is said to be subtle yet profound, shaping the very fabric of reality itself with a precision that echoes the intricacies of a grand cosmic symphony.

Whispers carried on the solar winds speak of a grand cosmic tapestry woven by the hands of the Elders, each thread representing a world, a civilization, and a moment in time. Some speculate that their purpose is to safeguard the delicate balance of the cosmos, ensuring that the forces of creation and destruction harmonize in a timeless dance of cosmic harmony. To seek their favor is to court enlightenment beyond mortal understanding, unlocking the universe's secrets hidden in the starlit void.

But caution is advised, for the Elders are beings of unfathomable power, their intentions veiled behind a veil of cosmic mystery. To gaze too deeply into the abyss of their existence is to risk losing oneself in the vastness of the unknown, forever adrift in the currents of the cosmic ocean. And so, the whispers of the Elders continue to beckon, a siren song of cosmic wonder that calls to those brave enough to seek the truths that lie beyond the Ice Wall.

- Unveiling the Enigmatic Life Beyond

In the frigid expanse beyond the Ice Wall lies a realm that defies conventional understanding - a domain teeming with enigmatic life forms that challenge our notions of existence. As explorers venture deeper into this frozen frontier, they encounter creatures unlike any found on the surface of Earth.

Beneath the icy surface, bioluminescent organisms illuminate the darkness, casting an ethereal glow that mesmerizes all who behold it. These mysterious beings, adapted to survive in the extreme conditions of the Antarctic depths, thrive in a world hidden from human eyes.

Among these elusive creatures are the ice-dwelling organisms that have evolved unique adaptations to survive in sub-zero temperatures. From resilient microorganisms to bizarre sea creatures, the diversity of life beyond the Ice Wall is captivating and baffling.

As researchers delve further into this enigmatic realm, they uncover intricate ecosystems that have developed in isolation for millennia. Each discovery sheds new light on the interconnected web of life that thrives in this harsh and unforgiving environment.

Yet, as we unravel the mysteries of the enigmatic life beyond, we are left with more questions than answers. How do these creatures endure the extreme cold? What secrets do they hold about the Earth's ancient past? And what implications do they have for our understanding of life itself?

The enigmatic life beyond the Ice Wall beckons us to explore, question, and contemplate the profound mysteries that lie at the edge of our known world. It is a place of wonder and discovery, where the boundaries of reality blur and the true essence of life reveals itself in all its mysterious beauty.

As explorers venture deeper into the frozen abyss, they encounter beings defying all known classifications. Strange, tentacled creatures move with a grace not seen on the surface, their iridescent bodies pulsating with otherworldly hues. These beings seem to possess a collective intelligence, communicating through unseen means that baffle even the most seasoned researchers.

In the depths of this hidden realm, time seems to lose its meaning, as ancient species coexist with newly evolved life forms in a delicate balance. Giant, translucent crustaceans drift serenely through the icy waters, their movements synchronized as if part of a grand dance choreographed by forces beyond human comprehension.

The air is thick with a palpable energy, as if the fabric of reality is thinner here, allowing glimpses into dimensions unknown to humanity. Whispers of long-forgotten myths and legends echo through the vast expanse as if the creatures are keepers of ancient knowledge that predates humanity.

As the explorers press on, drawn deeper into the mysteries of this enigmatic world, they feel a profound sense of awe and reverence for the beauty and complexity that lies before them. Each encounter with these wondrous beings leaves them humbled and inspired, their minds opened to the infinite possibilities beyond the confines of our known reality.

Impact on Earth's Paradigms

The discovery and exploration of the Ice Wall have sent shockwaves through the established paradigms of Earth's understanding. Scientists, theorists, and explorers alike have been forced to reevaluate their beliefs and assumptions in the face of this enigmatic barrier. Such a massive, impenetrable wall of ice challenges conventional notions of the Earth's geography and pushes the boundaries of what we thought we knew about our planet.

The implications of the Ice Wall's existence are far-reaching, impacting our understanding of the physical world and our perception of reality. The veil of mystery that shrouds the Ice Wall raises profound questions about our existence, the limits of human knowledge, and the hidden truths that lie beyond our grasp.

As humanity grapples with the implications of the Ice Wall, our paradigms must shift to accommodate the new realities that this discovery brings to light. The once-solid ground of our understanding is now called into question, and we face the daunting task of rebuilding our worldview from the ground up. The Ice Wall is a sentinel of change, a marker of a new human exploration and understanding era.

In the wake of this monumental discovery, we are forced to confront our limitations and biases, challenge the boundaries of our perception, and embrace the unknown with open minds and hearts. The Ice Wall is not just a physical boundary on the map; it is a symbolic boundary that separates what we know from what we have yet to discover. It is a reminder that the universe is vast, mysterious, and full of wonders waiting to be revealed.

The Ice Wall's sheer size and grandeur evokes a sense of awe and wonder in those who stand before it. Its towering walls of ice stretch endlessly in either direction, a testament to the power and beauty of the natural world. The intricate patterns and formations etched into its surface speak of a history and a story waiting to be uncovered.

The Ice Wall's presence challenges us to question our place in the cosmos, ponder the mysteries of existence, and seek the truths that lie beyond the confines of our current understanding. It beckons us to embark on a journey of exploration and discovery, push the boundaries of human knowledge, and embrace the unknown with courage and curiosity.

As we gaze upon the Ice Wall, we are reminded of the vastness and complexity of the universe, of the infinite possibilities that lie just beyond our reach. It reminds us that there is still so much left to explore, discover, and learn. The Ice Wall stands as a challenge, an invitation, a beacon of knowledge, and a symbol of the endless quest for understanding that drives us forward into the unknown.

- **Rupturing Reality's Perceptions**

Deep within the icy unknown lies a realm where perceptions of reality are shattered and remade. Beyond the Ice Wall, the boundaries of normality dissolve, unveiling a reality distorted by unseen powers.

As explorers venture further into this icy domain, they are confronted with sights and experiences that challenge everything they thought they knew. Their understanding crumbles in the face of the enigmatic revelations that the Ice Wall conceals.

Rupturing reality's perceptions, the Ice Wall acts as a catalyst for a profound shift in consciousness. It forces those who dare to approach its icy barrier to question the nature of the world around them and their place within it. Illusions are dispelled in the shadows cast by the towering wall of ice, and truth's long buried surface.

As the boundaries between the known and the unknown blur, those who venture beyond the Ice Wall find themselves caught in a whirlwind of conflicting truths and unanswered questions. Reality becomes a malleable construct shaped by the mysterious forces beyond the barrier.

In this realm of shattered perceptions, explorers must navigate a landscape where nothing is as it seems. Time bends and twists, space warps and distorts, and the very essence of reality is called into question. To journey beyond the Ice Wall is to embrace a new way of seeing the world that challenges the very fabric of existence and opens the door to infinite possibilities.

In the icy depths of the unknown, reality's perceptions are ruptured, and a new understanding emerges. It is a place where the boundaries of the mind are pushed to their limits and where the truth lies hidden beneath layers of mystery and wonder.

As the explorers delve deeper into the secrets of the Ice Wall, they unravel the intricate tapestry of existence itself. Whispers of ancient knowledge beckon to them from the swirling mists that dance around the icy barriers, urging them to probe further into the enigma of the unknown.

Each step forward is a step into the unknown, a journey into the heart of mysteries that have long eluded human understanding. The air seems to vibrate with a palpable energy, a sense of something vast and incomprehensible lurking just beyond reach.

And yet, despite the daunting challenges that lie ahead, the allure of discovery propels the explorers ever onward. Beyond the Ice Wall lies the unknown and the potential for a paradigm shift in how humanity perceives its place in the vast tapestry of the cosmos.

As the shadows lengthen and the icy winds howl, the explorers press on, driven by a thirst for knowledge that transcends the boundaries of fear and uncertainty. Beyond the Ice Wall, the mysteries of existence await, whispering promises of enlightenment and revelation to those brave enough to seek them out.

The depths of the frozen wasteland hold more than just chilling winds and icy landscapes; they harbor secrets as ancient as time itself. The ground beneath the explorers' feet seems to pulse with faint energy, as if the very earth is alive and aware of their presence.

Time becomes an elusive concept beyond the Ice Wall, where the boundaries between past, present, and future blur into a swirling vortex of possibilities. The explorers find themselves caught in a dance with time as moments stretch and contract in a kaleidoscope of fleeting glimpses.

In this frozen realm, reality is a fluid and mutable entity, and the laws of physics bend and twist to accommodate the mysterious forces at play. The explorers witness phenomena defying logic and reason, questioning existence.

As they journey deeper into this enigmatic domain, the explorers sense a presence watching them, an ancient and primal consciousness that seems to permeate the surrounding air. Whispers of forgotten truths drift on the icy winds, tantalizing them with glimpses of knowledge long lost to the annals of time.

The Ice Wall is a sentinel between worlds, a gateway to dimensions beyond human comprehension. It beckons the explorers with promises of profound insight and enlightenment, drawing them ever closer to the heart of the mysteries buried within its frozen depths.

With each step forward, the explorers feel a sense of both trepidation and exhilaration, as if they are on the brink of discovering something that will change the course of history itself. The air crackles with anticipation, and the shadows seem to dance in anticipation of the revelations that await beyond the Ice Wall.

- Ice Wall's Revelation on Humanity

As explorers press on beyond the foreboding Ice Wall, the secrets of the frozen expanse continue to unfurl before them in a mesmerizing display of ancient mysteries and enigmatic wonders. As they traverse the frigid terrain, they stumble upon structures that defy all expectations–towering spires of ice that seem to pulsate with a faint, ethereal glow, as if infused with a power long forgotten by the world above.

In the heart of this frozen labyrinth, they discover intricate carvings etched into the ice walls, depicting scenes of a bygone era where technology and magic intertwined in a harmonious dance. Symbols that resonate with primal energy whisper ancient truths to those brave enough to decipher their enigmatic language, hinting when the boundaries between the material and the metaphysical were blurred beyond recognition.

As they delve further into this icy realm, the explorers uncover artifacts that speak of a civilization far more advanced than any previously known to humanity. Devices of unknown purpose, adorned with runes that shimmer with an otherworldly light, challenge the very foundations of their understanding of science and existence. Could these relics hold the key to unlocking a power that has long lain dormant within the hearts of humankind?

But perhaps the most awe-inspiring of all is the revelation of a hidden library deep within the bowels of the Ice Wall. Within its frozen chambers lie tomes filled with knowledge beyond comprehension, detailing the intricate workings of the universe and the interconnectedness of all things. As the explorers pore over these ancient texts, a sense of awe and reverence washes over them, for they realize they stand on the threshold of a profound transformation–individually and collectively.

In the calm stillness of the library, a whisper stirs among the pages, carrying with it a prophecy as old as time itself. It speaks of a chosen few who will rise to unlock the ancient power slumbering within the Ice Wall, restoring balance to a world teetering on the brink of chaos. As the words resonate deep within their souls, the explorers understand their journey is not just one of discovery but of destiny–a journey that will forever alter the course of human history and awaken a latent potential that lies dormant within us all.

The implications of this discovery ripple through the expedition team, stirring a mix of awe, excitement, and trepidation. They now face a choice: to continue their quest, risking the unknown dangers that lie ahead, or to retreat to the safety of the familiar world they once knew. But deep within their hearts, a fire has been kindled–a spark of curiosity and determination that propels them forward, drawing them ever closer to the heart of the Ice Wall and the secrets that await them there.

As they prepare to embark on the next leg of their journey, the explorers ponder the significance of their discovery. Could the ancient power of the Ice Wall hold the key to unlocking humanity's potential for greatness? Or does it harbor a darker, more insidious force threatening to consume all who dare to seek it? Only time will tell as they set forth into the unknown, their destiny entwined with the mysteries of the Ice Wall and the secrets it guards within its frozen heart.

- Shifting the Earth's Axis of Understanding

In the depths of the unknown realms beyond the Ice Wall, explorers are confronted with a convergence of enigmatic forces that challenge the very fabric of reality. As they press further into the uncharted territories, the boundaries between the physical and metaphysical blur, revealing a tapestry of interconnected energies pulsating with cosmic significance.

The shifting of the Earth's axis of understanding takes on a profound resonance as explorers witness the intricate dance of celestial bodies and unseen forces that govern the cosmic symphony. Each discovery and revelation unfolds like a chapter in a cosmic epic, weaving together threads of knowledge and mystery in a tapestry of infinite complexity.

As explorers navigate the multidimensional landscape beyond the Ice Wall, they are confronted with the profound realization that the universe is not merely a collection of disparate elements, but a harmonious whole interconnected by invisible threads of energy and consciousness. Every step taken into the unknown leads to a deeper understanding of the interconnectedness of all things, prompting a reevaluation of humanity's place in the grand tapestry of existence.

The mysteries beyond the Ice Wall beckon explorers to delve deeper into the recesses of their minds, inviting them to embrace the transformative power of self-discovery and inner growth. As they grapple with the unfathomable truths that unfold before them, explorers are compelled to confront their limitations and expand their consciousness to encompass the vastness of the cosmos.

Through exploring the unknown realms beyond the Ice Wall, explorers are not merely uncovering new landscapes and phenomena, but embarking on a journey of soulful evolution and enlightenment. The shifting of the Earth's axis of understanding becomes a metaphor for the transformative power of exploration and discovery, guiding humanity towards a deeper connection with the mysteries of the universe and the infinite possibilities that await us in the boundless depths of the cosmos.

Unveiling the Veil of Reality

As the intrepid explorers ventured deeper into the frozen expanse beyond the Ice Wall, a sense of foreboding crept into their hearts. The icy landscape seemed to whisper ancient secrets, its frozen tendrils reaching out to ensnare the unwary traveler. Each step forward felt like a descent into the unknown, a journey into the heart of darkness hidden beneath the ice.

The explorers' minds were consumed with questions that echoed through the icy corridors of their thoughts. What mysteries lay buried in the frozen depths before them? What truths awaited those who dared to delve into the snowy abyss of the unknown? With each passing moment, the veil of reality that had once masked the secrets of the Ice Wall grew ever thinner, revealing glimpses of a world that defied comprehension.

The shards of ice that littered the landscape seemed to pulse with life, their crystalline structures vibrating with otherworldly energy. It was as if the ice itself was a living entity, a repository of knowledge that had been locked away for millennia. The explorers felt a deep sense of unease as they realized they stood on the threshold of a reality far beyond their understanding.

As they pressed on, the shadows that danced on the icy surface seemed to take on their own life, twisting and contorting in unnatural shapes. Whispers of long-forgotten truths echoed through the snowy corridors, tantalizing the explorers with the promise of enlightenment and peril in equal measure.

But despite the dangers lurking around every corner, the explorers remained resolute in their quest for truth. Their will was like a beacon of light in the swirling darkness, guiding them forward into the unknown, for they knew that the ultimate revelation awaited them, a revelation that would shake the very foundations of their beliefs and redefine the boundaries of reality itself.

The icy expanse stretched out before them like a vast, frozen tapestry, shimmering with an otherworldly beauty that belied the dangers lurking within its depths. The explorers marveled at the intricacy of the ice formations surrounding them, their crystalline structures weaving a tale of eons past.

As they journeyed more profoundly into the frozen wasteland, the temperature dropped sharply, biting at their exposed skin and seeping into their bones. The icy silence of the landscape was broken only by the soft crunch of their boots on the frozen ground, a stark reminder of their isolation in this frigid wilderness.

They stumbled upon ancient ruins buried beneath the ice, their weathered stone surfaces hinting at a forgotten civilization. Symbols etched into the icy walls spoke of a language lost to time, their meaning shrouded in mystery. The explorers felt a sense of reverence for the remnants of a culture that had once thrived in this desolate land.

A sense of unease settled over them as they delved deeper into the ruins. Shadows flitted at the edges of their vision, whispers echoed through the icy corridors, and a chill wind carried the echoes of long-dead voices. The explorers pressed on, driven by a hunger for knowledge that transcended their fear.

And so, the explorers continued their journey into the heart of the Ice Wall, unaware of the profound truths and ancient dangers that awaited them in the frozen expanse beyond.

- Quest for Truth Beyond the Ice Wall

As the explorers pressed onward, the landscape shifted from jagged ice formations to a desolate expanse where the air crackled with otherworldly energy. The icy winds whispered eerie melodies that seemed to echo from the depths of time, stirring a primal sense of wonder and fear in their hearts.

The further they journeyed beyond the Ice Wall, the more apparent it became that they were entering a realm unlike anything they had ever encountered. Strange symbols etched into the ice seemed to pulse with a faint, ethereal light, casting an eerie glow over the frozen landscape and hinting at the presence of ancient forces at play.

As they ventured deeper into the heart of the unknown, the explorers encountered structures unlike any they had seen before. Massive ice spires jutted up from the frozen ground, their crystalline surfaces reflecting the pale light of a sun that never seemed to rise fully. Within the depths of these icy fortresses, they uncovered chambers adorned with intricate carvings depicting scenes from a forgotten history, hinting at a civilization long lost to the unforgiving embrace of the ice.

Despite the harsh conditions and the ever-present sense of foreboding, the explorers pressed on, their minds consumed by the compelling mystery that lay just beyond their reach. They knew they were on the cusp of a revelation that could change the course of history, driving them forward with a sense of purpose that transcended their physical challenges.

And then, as they reached the heart of the frozen realm, they beheld a sight that took their breath away—before they stood a towering monolith of ice, its surface shimmering with a strange, otherworldly energy that seemed to pulse with a life of its own. As they approached, they could feel a deep thrum resonating through the very core of their beings, drawing them closer to the enigmatic structure that held the key to the mysteries of the Ice Wall.

With trembling hands, they reached out to touch the icy surface of the monolith. As their fingers made contact, a surge of energy surged through them, filling their minds with visions of a world beyond comprehension. They saw civilizations rise and fall, cataclysms that reshaped the very fabric of reality, and a cosmic dance of forces that transcended space and time.

In that moment of revelation, they knew they had uncovered only a fraction of the truths that lay beyond the Ice Wall and that the journey they had embarked upon was just the beginning of an odyssey that would forever alter their understanding of the world and their place within it. And so, with hearts filled with awe and wonder, they gazed upon the monolith and knew their quest for truth had only begun.

- Truth Seekers in the Frozen Unknown

The truth seekers gathered around the campfire, their faces illuminated by the flickering flames that danced against the icy backdrop of the Arctic landscape. Dr. Hartley, her eyes alight with a fervor born of discovery, shared her latest findings with the group, each word carrying a weight of significance that echoed through the barren expanse.

"These symbols," she began, tracing the intricate patterns etched into the ice with a gloved finger, "bear a striking resemblance to ancient texts I've studied in my years of research. But there's something more to them, a hidden meaning that eludes even the most seasoned scholars."

The truth seekers leaned in closer, their breath forming frosty clouds in the frigid air, as Dr. Hartley delved deeper into the mysteries of the Ice Wall. She spoke of legends passed down through generations, whispered tales of lost civilizations that thrived in the frozen wasteland long before the first humans set foot on its icy shores.

As the night wore on, the group braved the biting cold to explore the base of the Ice Wall, their footsteps echoing against the frozen ground like a heartbeat pulsing through the ancient ice. Shadows danced across the towering structure, casting a cloak of mystery over its pristine surface as if guarding the universe's secrets within its icy embrace.

Dr. Hartley kneeled before an elaborate symbol, her scholarly gaze piercing through the layers of ice to unravel the hidden truths beneath. She traced the lines with a reverence reserved for the sacred, feeling a surge of energy emanating from the very ice itself as if the knowledge of the ages was waiting to be unlocked by those willing to seek it out.

As the first light of dawn broke over the horizon, casting a pink hue over the icy landscape, the truth seekers stood united before the Ice Wall, their hearts filled with a sense of wonder and purpose. For beyond this formidable barrier lay a realm of untold possibilities and infinite knowledge, beckoning them to take the next step in their journey of discovery. They were on the brink of uncovering a truth that transcended time and space, a truth that would forever change the course of their lives.

- The Everlasting Search for Enlightenment

In the frigid expanse beyond the Ice Wall, a symphony of silence envelops the intrepid explorers who brave the icy wastelands for enlightenment. Each footfall reverberates through the frozen landscape, a testament to the tenacity and determination that drives them forward into the unknown.

As they venture deeper into the icy mysteries, the boundaries between reality and imagination blur, casting a surreal enchantment over the desolate terrain. Shadows dance across the frozen expanse, whispering ancient secrets etched into the very fabric of the ice. Symbols of forgotten civilizations emerge from the frost, their meanings shrouded in the mists of time, beckoning the explorers to unlock the mysteries buried beneath the frozen surface.

Amidst the endless expanse of white, the explorers discover a labyrinthine network of ice caverns, their crystalline walls pulsating with an otherworldly luminescence. Time seems to lose all meaning within these ethereal chambers, and the explorers find themselves caught in a web of cosmic forces that transcend the boundaries of mortal understanding.

Echoes of a distant past resonate through the icy corridors, carrying with them the whispers of long-forgotten voices and the echoes of civilizations long vanished. A sense of awe and reverence consumes the explorers, their minds expanding to encompass the vastness of the universe and the interconnectedness of all things.

As they press further into the depths of the icy unknown, a profound realization dawns upon them—that in their quest for enlightenment, they are not merely searching for answers to questions of the mind but embarking on a journey of the soul. The icy wastelands become a crucible of transformation, forging them into beings of higher consciousness, attuned to the cosmic energies that flow through the universe.

Amidst the shimmering icicles that hang like crystalline stalactites from the frozen ceilings, the explorers uncover ancient artifacts of a bygone era–relics of a civilization long forgotten, their purpose and significance lost to the ravages of time. Each artifact tells a story, a fragment of a narrative that stretches back through the eons, illuminating the paths taken by those who came before.

As they piece together the fragments of this enigmatic puzzle, the explorers feel drawn ever deeper into the mysteries of the ice, their hearts and minds intertwined with the cosmic energies that pulse through the frozen landscape. They sense they are on the verge of a profound revelation, a moment of clarity that will forever alter their understanding of the universe and their place within it.

And so, bathed in the numinous glow of the ice, the explorers continue their eternal quest for enlightenment, their souls ablaze with the fire of discovery and transformation. Beyond the Ice Wall lies not just a realm of frost and shadow but a gateway to a higher reality, where the mysteries of the universe unfold in all their infinite beauty and complexity, waiting to be revealed to those with the courage and the wisdom to seek them out.

Epilogue: Shadows in the Perpetual Ice

As the journey beyond the Ice Wall draws to a close, one cannot help but reflect on the profound impact of the frozen frontier on the human psyche. The shadows cast by the perpetual ice leave an indelible mark on those who dare to venture into its icy embrace. Each step taken in the vast expanse of the unknown echoes with the whispers of ancient mysteries and enigmatic secrets.

The literal and metaphorical shadows play tricks on the mind, blurring the line between reality and illusion. Long shadows stretch across the icy terrain as the sun wanes in the frigid landscape, painting a picture of solitude and introspection. In these moments of quiet contemplation, the true nature of the Ice Wall reveals itself, a place where time stands still and the boundaries of perception are forever blurred.

Beyond the veil of ice lies a realm of endless possibilities, where the echoes of the past reverberate through the ages. Shadows dance across the frozen landscape, weaving tales of forgotten civilizations and lost explorers. Each gust of wind carries the whispers of those who have come before, their stories etched in the icy expanse for eternity.

In the perpetual ice, shadows take on a life of their own, morphing and shifting with the changing light. They remind us of the transient nature of existence, a stark contrast to the timeless beauty of the frozen frontier. Standing on the unknown threshold, surrounded by shadows and ice, we are reminded of our mortality and the impermanence of all things.

And yet, amidst the shadows and ice, a sense of awe and wonder pervades the soul. The perpetual ice is critical to unlocking humanity's greatest mysteries, offering a glimpse into the unknown and the unfathomable. As we bid farewell to the shadows in the perpetual ice, we carry a newfound sense of purpose and a deeper understanding of the world.

The sheer magnitude of the Ice Wall commands respect and reverence. It is a towering monument to the power of nature and the resilience of the human spirit. Its icy tendrils reach out like the fingers of a titan, grasping at the sky in a timeless dance of creation and destruction. It is a place where the boundaries of reality blur, where the laws of physics seem to bend and twist in a symphony of chaos and beauty.

As we gaze upon the icy expanse before us, we cannot help but feel a deep connection to something greater than ourselves. The shadows that dance across the frozen landscape remind us of the intricate tapestry of existence, a delicate balance of light and dark, of life and death. In the stillness of the frozen frontier, we find solace knowing that we are but small pieces in a vast and infinite puzzle, each with our part to play in the grand scheme of creation.

And so, as we bid farewell to the shadows in the perpetual ice and turn our gaze back towards the horizon, we carry a newfound sense of purpose and wonder. The echoes of the past linger in the icy air, whispering their secrets to those willing to listen. In the silence of the frozen frontier, we find a profound sense of peace and understanding, a reminder that in the shadows of the perpetual ice, beauty, and truth are waiting to be discovered.

As the explorers prepare to leave the Ice Wall behind, they feel grateful for the lessons learned and the mysteries uncovered in this frozen realm. The shadows of the perpetual ice will forever linger in their memories, a reminder of the fragility and resilience of the human spirit in the face of nature's vast and unfathomable power. And so, with a last glance at the icy expanse, the adventurers turn their backs on the shadows and set forth towards new horizons, carrying with them the wisdom and experience gained in the land beyond the Wall.

- Reflecting on Trails of Ice and Shadows

As the explorers continued their journey across the icy expanse, the landscape seemed to shift and morph around them, revealing glimpses of a forgotten world. Each step on the treacherous terrain carried them deeper into the heart of the frozen realm, where time appeared to stand still.

Whispers of ancient legends and tales of lost civilizations echoed through the icy corridors, their voices haunting the explorers' thoughts as they pressed onward. The stories spoke of a time when powerful beings roamed these frozen lands, shaping the ice and snow with their otherworldly presence. Some whispered of a great city buried beneath the ice, its spires reaching towards the sky in defiance of the frigid prison that held it captive.

The explorers found themselves captivated by the mystical allure of the frozen realm, drawn to the enigmatic beauty surrounding them. It was as if the ice held a secret longing to be discovered, to shed light on the forgotten truths hidden within its crystalline depths.

Lost in the silence of the icy wilderness, the explorers grappled with the profound weight of their discoveries. It was not just the physical challenges of their expedition that tested their resolve, but the enigmatic truths that lay veiled behind the curtain of ice, begging to be unraveled.

The shadows cast by the towering ice peaks took on their own life, swirling and dancing in ethereal patterns that spoke of secrets hidden within the frozen maze. Each gust of wind carried a whisper of the past, a faint echo of a time long gone but not forgotten.

With each breath drawn in the frigid air, the explorers felt a sense of reverence for the frozen landscape surrounding them. It was a reminder of the boundless mysteries that awaited those who dared to venture into the shadows and embrace the enigmatic beauty of the icy frontier, where the echoes of forgotten truths reverberated through the frozen expanse.

As they pondered the vast mysteries that lay before them, the explorers felt a deep sense of connection to the enigmatic beauty of the ice wall. It stood as a silent sentinel, guarding the secrets of the frozen realm and beckoning those brave enough to peer into its depths and uncover the hidden truths buried within the icy fortress.

- Beyond the Veil of Ice: Forever Mysteries

The explorers stood at the edge of the Ice Wall, their breaths forming misty clouds in the frigid air. As they gazed out into the abyss of eternal mysteries, a sense of insignificance washed over them like a wave crashing against the shore. The silence was deafening, broken only by the faint echoes of their heartbeats reverberating in the vast expanse.

In the distance, shadowy figures seemed to dance on the surface of the ice, their movements fluid and ethereal. The explorers squinted, trying to make sense of the swirling patterns that seemed to defy logic and reason. Were they hallucinations brought on by the extreme cold or manifestations of a reality beyond their comprehension?

The ice seemed to pulse with strange energy, like a living entity with secrets to keep. The shimmering surface reflected the pale sunlight in a mesmerizing display of colors, creating an otherworldly spectacle that mesmerized the explorers. They felt as if they were standing on the threshold of a realm where time held no sway, where the boundaries between dream and reality blurred into indistinct shadows.

As they delved deeper into the mysteries of the Ice Wall, they uncovered fragments of forgotten history, whispers of a civilization long lost to the annals of time. Ancient symbols etched into the ice seemed to tell a story of a bygone era, a narrative of a people who had once thrived in this barren landscape. The explorers traced the intricate patterns with reverent fingers, feeling a sense of connection to a past erased by the relentless march of time.

But as they delved further into the heart of the ice, they encountered phenomena that defied explanation. Wisps of ghostly figures flitted at the corners of their vision, disappearing as quickly as they had appeared. The explorers hesitated, unsure if what they witnessed was real or merely a trick of the mind. Reality seemed to warp and twist in this surreal landscape, leaving them grasping for a foothold in a shifting world of uncertainty.

And yet, despite the myriad mysteries surrounding them, the explorers felt a profound sense of peace settle over their hearts. They realized some enigmas were not meant to be unraveled and that some truths were too vast for mortal minds to comprehend. As they turned away from the Ice Wall, their souls heavy with the weight of all they had seen, they knew they had glimpsed a glimpse of the infinite complexity of the universe, a fleeting moment of understanding in a sea of eternal mysteries.

The wind picked up, carrying a haunting melody that seemed to echo ancient chants from a time long forgotten. The explorers shivered from the cold and the inexplicable sense of being watched by unseen eyes. They quickened their pace, eager to leave behind the enigmatic realm of the Ice Wall and return to the safety of familiar landscapes.

But as they retraced their steps, a sudden rumbling beneath their feet brought them to a halt. The ground trembled, causing fissures to appear in the ice, like scars on the face of a sleeping giant. The explorers exchanged uneasy glances, realizing they may have awoken forces beyond their control.

Just as they were about to flee, a blinding light erupted from the depths of the fissures, bathing the landscape in a surreal glow. The explorers shielded their eyes, unable to comprehend the magnitude of the spectacle unfolding before them. And then, as quickly as it had appeared, the light vanished, leaving a sense of awe and wonder lingering in the air like a whisper from a forgotten dream.

They knew then that their journey to the Ice Wall had not been in vain. They had touched upon something greater than themselves, transcending the boundaries of time and space. As they made their way back to civilization, their minds abuzz with what they had witnessed, they carried a newfound reverence for the mysteries of the universe and a renewed sense of humility in the unknown's face.

- Embracing the Eternal Journey

As we pressed onward, the chilling embrace of the Ice Wall enveloped us in a stark reminder of our mortality. The towering walls of ice seemed to whisper tales of ancient civilizations long forgotten, their secrets locked away within the frozen fortress that stood as a testament to nature's unfathomable power.

The shifting shadows played tricks on our minds, conjuring illusions of phantoms and specters that danced just beyond our reach. Each breath we took hung in the frigid air like a tangible echo of our fleeting existence, starkly contrasting the serenity that pervaded the icy expanse.

The very essence of the Ice Wall seemed to pulsate with mysterious energy as if the ice itself harbored a consciousness that transcended the boundaries of mere physicality. We were but transient visitors in this realm of primordial ice, our presence a fleeting moment in the vast tapestry of existence that stretched before us like an eternal enigma waiting to be unraveled.

As we ventured deeper into the heart of the Ice Wall, the whispers of ancient wisdom grew louder, reverberating through the frozen corridors and resonating deep within our beings. We could almost sense unseen forces guiding our steps, leading us toward a revelation that defied comprehension yet beckoned us with a magnetic allure.

The intricacies of the ice formations revealed a story written in a language older than time itself, a narrative of creation and destruction, rebirth and renewal that unfolded before our eyes with a mesmerizing beauty that transcended mere aesthetics. Each crystalline structure told a tale of cosmic proportions that resonated with the essence of our existence and connected us to a more profound truth hidden within the icy depths.

As we stood on the threshold of enlightenment, gazing into the infinite expanse of the Ice Wall, a profound sense of awe and reverence washed over us, humbling us in the presence of forces beyond our understanding. We were but transient beings in a world that existed long before us and would endure long after we were gone, a world of unfathomable complexity and unfettered beauty that defied all attempts at rational explanation.

At that moment, as the icy winds whispered their final secrets and the frozen expanse stretched out before us in all its silent majesty, we knew we had glimpsed but a fraction of the mysteries that lay hidden within the heart of the Ice Wall, and that our journey was far from over.

Appendix: Further Explorations of the Unknown

- As our expedition delves beyond the Ice Wall, the landscape becomes increasingly otherworldly, with jagged ice formations looming overhead and eerie mists swirling around us. The air grows colder, biting at our exposed skin and seeping into our bones, a constant reminder of the harshness of this unforgiving environment.

- We push on, our determination fueled by an insatiable thirst for knowledge and discovery. The stark beauty of the icy wilderness captivates us, its haunting serenity a stark contrast to the relentless brutality of the elements. Every step we take feels like a journey into the unknown, each new vista revealing a landscape that defies comprehension.

- Ancient ruins stand as silent sentinels of a forgotten time, their weathered stones bearing witness to passing millennia. We sift through the debris, piecing together fragments of a civilization long lost to the ravages of time. Symbols and glyphs etched into the stones hint at a culture steeped in mystery and ritual, their meanings obscure.

- The flora and fauna of this frozen realm are like nothing we have ever encountered. Strange, otherworldly plants cling to rocky crevices, their vibrant hues standing out starkly against the monochromatic backdrop of ice and snow. Animals adapted to the harsh conditions of the tundra roam the landscape, their survival a testament to the resilience of life in even the most inhospitable of environments.

- As we delve deeper into the heart of this frozen wilderness, we are struck by the profound sense of insignificance that washes over us. In the vast expanse of the icy wasteland, we are but fleeting specks of life, insignificant in the grand tapestry of existence. Yet, as we uncover the remnants of ancient civilizations and unravel the mysteries of this enigmatic realm, we are reminded of the enduring legacy of those who came before us, their stories woven into the very fabric of the land itself.

- Resonating Echoes of the Ice Wall

As the first light of dawn painted the horizon in hues of soft pink and gold, the explorers stirred from their fitful slumber, their dreams haunted by visions of the Ice Wall that loomed ominously before them. The elder's tale from the night before whispered through their minds like an elusive melody, enticing them with promises of forgotten wonders and untold mysteries waiting to be unraveled.

One of the group's younger members, a fervent scholar with eyes alight with curiosity, took it upon himself to begin a meticulous examination of the ancient glyphs and markings etched into the surface of the Ice Wall. His fingers traced the intricate patterns, feeling the chill of the ice seeping into his skin as he sought to decipher the cryptic messages that had long baffled even the most seasoned of explorers.

As the day unfurled its silken tendrils across the frozen landscape, the explorers gathered around the scholar, their breath forming frosty clouds in the frigid air as they listened intently to his findings. He spoke of a lost civilization that had once thrived beyond the Ice Wall, a society steeped in knowledge and wisdom far beyond the comprehension of the present age.

According to the scholar's research, this enigmatic civilization had harnessed the elemental forces of ice and snow, shaping them into tools of great power and mystery. They had crafted intricate sculptures and artifacts imbued with a magic that defied rational explanation, their creations standing as silent sentinels to a time long past.

The scholar's words ignited a spark of hope within the hearts of the explorers, a glimmer of possibility that perhaps, with patience and perseverance, they could unlock the secrets of the Ice Wall and uncover the truths that had eluded them for so long.

And so, with renewed determination and a shared sense of purpose, the intrepid band of adventurers set out once more towards the towering barrier of ice, their eyes fixed on the shimmering expanse that held the key to a world of wonders waiting to be revealed.

- Prolonging the Quest for Knowledge

Within the boundless and relentless frozen domain, an eternal quest for knowledge that transcends time and space persists. From ancient tales to modern science, humanity's curiosity to explore the frozen world remains unwavering. This insatiable hunger for understanding has sent explorers on perilous journeys across treacherous glaciers, delving into the icy depths to uncover ancient truths hidden from sight.

The frozen expanse, with its towering glaciers and glistening ice formations, serves as a canvas for humanity's collective yearning to grasp the unknown and unlock the secrets shrouded in frost. Through the ages, adventurers and scientists alike have braved the harsh elements and ventured into the heart of the icy wilderness, driven by a shared desire to expand the boundaries of human knowledge.

As we stand on the precipice of discovery, gazing out into the frozen horizon, we are reminded of the infinite possibilities in the uncharted territories that lie beyond. Pursuing knowledge is not merely a quest for answers but a journey of self-discovery, a reflection of our innate curiosity and determination to push the boundaries of what is known and delve deeper into the mysteries beneath the icy surface.

In this timeless pursuit, we are bound by a common thread that links us to the explorers of old and the visionaries of the future, united in our shared quest to unravel the enigmas of the icy realm and shed light on the dark corners of the unknown. As we venture into the frozen expanse, we are driven by the belief that the journey itself is a testament to the resilience of the human spirit and our unyielding determination to seek the truths that lie hidden in the icy depths.

And so, we press on, guided by the flickering light of knowledge that beckons us forward, illuminating the path ahead with the promise of discovery and the realization that pursuiting knowledge is not merely a destination but a journey of endless possibilities stretching out before us, waiting to be explored and embraced.

As the wind howls through the icy canyons and the shimmering auroras dance across the polar sky, we are reminded of the profound interconnectedness of all life on Earth and the delicate balance that sustains our existence in this frozen wilderness. With its stark beauty and unforgiving terrain, the frozen realm holds within its icy grasp the secrets of our past and the potential for our future. The ancient ice sheets, with each layer a time capsule of a bygone era, offer a glimpse into the ever-evolving history of our planet and the profound changes that have shaped the world we inhabit today.

In the depths of the frozen expanse, where the ice whispers ancient tales, and the glaciers groan with the weight of millennia, we are drawn inexorably forward into the unknown, propelled by a thirst for knowledge that transcends the confines of our individual experiences. Each step taken in the icy wilderness is a testament to our collective commitment to understanding the world and the mysteries that lie beyond our reach.

As we navigate the frozen labyrinth, charting a course through the icy valleys and across the windswept plains, we are humbled by the vastness of the landscape and the enormity of the challenges that lie ahead. Yet faced with such adversity, we are encouraged by the shared purpose that unites us in our quest for discovery, forging a bond that transcends the boundaries of language and culture.

Amidst the endless expanse of ice and snow, we are reminded of the fragility of our existence and the importance of preserving the natural wonders surrounding us. With each discovery made in the frozen realm, we gain a deeper appreciation for the intricate web of life that sustains us and a renewed sense of wonder at the complexities of the natural world. And so, we continue our journey into the heart of the icy wilderness, guided by the unwavering light of knowledge that illuminates our path and beckons us ever forward into the unknown.

- Beyond the Book's Final Pages

As the explorers stood before the towering Ice Wall, they felt awe and wonder. The enormity of the barrier before them was staggering, stretching far beyond the reach of mortal vision. It was said that beyond this icy fortress lay a realm of untold mysteries, a place where the very fabric of reality seemed to warp and twist in ways that defied human understanding.

Whispers from ancient texts spoke of a hidden world beyond the Ice Wall, a realm where time flowed differently, where the laws of physics themselves seemed to bend and contort in ways that challenged the very nature of existence. Some speculated that this mysterious land was home to beings of unimaginable power and wisdom, while others believed it to be a desolate wasteland devoid of life.

But the explorer, undeterred by the unknown dangers that may lie ahead, felt a deep longing to uncover the truth that lay beyond. With each step closer to the imposing barrier, a sense of anticipation and trepidation mingled within their heart. What secrets awaited them on the other side? What wonders and terrors would they encounter in this uncharted realm?

As they pressed their palm against the icy surface, faint energy seemed to hum beneath their touch, as if the wall held a secret heartbeat, pulsing with the rhythm of an unseen world. It was an irresistible sensation, a promise of the extraordinary and the forbidden that lay just beyond their reach.

And so, with a deep breath and a steely resolve, the explorer took their first steps towards the Ice Wall, their fate intertwined with the mysteries that awaited them in the realm beyond. The journey had only begun, and the true adventure was yet to unfold in a tapestry of discovery and revelation that would leave an indelible mark on their soul.

As they gazed ahead, the explorer knew that beyond the Ice Wall, a realm of endless possibilities awaited, beckoning them to unravel its secrets and unlock the truths hidden within the unknown's icy heart.

The icy wall loomed before them, its surface glistening in the moon's pale light. Each crack and crevice seemed to hold a story, a tale of the countless ages since its creation. The explorer couldn't help but feel a sense of reverence for the ancient structure, a monument to the unfathomable forces that had shaped this frozen landscape.

The surrounding air grew colder as they continued, biting at their exposed skin with a relentless chill. But the explorer pressed on, driven by a sense of curiosity and determination that burned within their soul. They knew that the answers they sought lay just beyond this formidable barrier, waiting to be discovered in the hidden realm that lay beyond.

With a last surge of resolve, the explorer reached out and placed both hands against the icy surface of the wall. A surge of energy coursed through their veins, a primal connection to the mysteries that lay beyond. They closed their eyes and focused their mind, searching for a way to breach this impregnable fortress and uncover the secrets that lay hidden within.

And then, as if in response to their silent plea, a faint whisper echoed through the icy barrier, a voice from the other side beckoning them forward. It was a voice filled with ancient wisdom and untold knowledge, a guide to the wonders and perils that awaited in the realm beyond.

With a renewed sense of purpose, the explorer pushed forward, their heart filled with fear and excitement. The unknown lay before them, a realm of endless possibilities and unimaginable wonders waiting to be explored. As they took their first steps beyond the Ice Wall, they knew their journey was only beginning, a voyage into the heart of mystery and discovery that would forever change the course of their destiny.

Glossary of Enigmatic Terms

In the world of the Ice Wall, where mysteries and wonders abound, the lexicon of secrets continues to unravel before those who dare to delve deeper. Beyond the surface definitions lie layers of meaning that reveal the true nature of this frozen enigma. The Frostfire, that elusive essence that pulses within the Ice Wall's icy heart, is not merely a combination of ice and fire but a magical force that defies comprehension. It is said that Frostfire holds the key to unlocking the ancient enchantments that bind the Ice Wall together, a power that has been revered and feared by all who have encountered it.

The Whispers of the Ancients, those haunting echoes of a forgotten time, are more than mere sounds carried on the wind. They are fragments of a lost history, fragmented memories of a civilization long gone but not entirely forgotten. Those who have listened closely to the whispers claim to have glimpsed visions of a time when the Ice Wall was not the impenetrable barrier it is today, but a realm of beauty and wonder where kingdoms rose and fell like the shifting glaciers.

The Crystalline Veil, with its ethereal glow and sharp edges that cut through the icy air, is not just a physical barrier but a symbol of the Ice Wall's power and mystery. Legend has it that the Crystalline Veil was woven by ancient sorcerers using strands of Frostfire and enchanted ice, creating a boundary separating the known world from the unknown depths of the Ice Wall's inner sanctum. Those who have gazed upon the shimmering beauty of the Crystalline Veil are said to have been left spellbound, unable to tear their eyes away from its mesmerizing presence.

And then there is the Eternal Frost, the stony heart of the Ice Wall that has always held sway over the land. It is a reminder of the unyielding nature of the ice, a force that knows no mercy and shows no favoritism. The Eternal Frost whispers of a time when the world was locked in an eternal winter, when life struggled to survive in the icy grip of an unforgiving landscape. Those who brave the chill of the Eternal Frost are tested to their limits, their resolve and courage pushed to the breaking point as they seek to uncover the truths buried beneath the frozen surface.

As we navigate the depths of the lexicon of the Ice Wall, we are confronted with a language that speaks of ancient truths and hidden knowledge. Each term, each definition, is a piece of the puzzle that, when assembled, reveals a tapestry of secrets that have been guarded for centuries. The Ice Wall whispers its enigmas to those brave enough to listen, inviting them to unlock the mysteries buried within its icy embrace. As we continue to explore the depths of this enigmatic language, we find ourselves drawn ever closer to the heart of the Ice Wall and its secrets.

- Definitions Shrouded in Mystery

The lexicon of secrets surrounding the Ice Wall is a captivating tapestry woven with threads of mystery and intrigue, beckoning explorers and scholars alike to unravel its enigmatic depths. As we delve further into the meanings behind words like "Ecliptic Anomaly," "Polar Inversion," and "Subzero Veil," we uncover layers of complexity that hint at a reality far beyond our conventional understanding.

The term "Ecliptic Anomaly" speaks of a disruption in the celestial pathways, a deviation from the natural order that governs the movement of heavenly bodies across the sky. Could this anomaly be linked to the peculiar phenomena observed near the Ice Wall, where shadows lengthen unexpectedly and stars seem to dance with an otherworldly grace?

"Polar Inversion" suggests a radical shift in the fundamental forces that shape our world, a reordering of magnetic fields and gravitational pulls that defy our preconceived notions of stability and equilibrium. What cataclysmic event could have caused such an inversion, and what implications does it hold for the regions beyond the Ice Wall?

And then there is the enigmatic "Subzero Veil," a term that conjures images of a frigid barrier separating known reality from uncharted realms of ice and mystery. Is this veil a physical boundary, a metaphysical barrier, or perhaps a state of mind that must be crossed before one can grasp the true nature of the Ice Wall and the secrets it guards?

Delving deeper into the lore of the Ice Wall, whispers among ancient manuscripts speak of a time before the celestial dance above the ice-bound realm was not as it is now. Legends tell of a cosmic event, a convergence of forces that shattered the fabric of reality and left in its wake the frozen expanse we now know as the Ice Wall. Could the Ecliptic Anomaly be a lingering echo of this ancient upheaval, a haunting reminder of a world long past?

As we contemplate the implications of the Polar Inversion, scholars debate the nature of magnetic and gravitational anomalies that plague the regions near the Ice Wall. Some theorize that these disruptions signify a hidden power, a force that lies dormant beneath the icy surface, waiting to be awakened by those brave enough to seek its secrets. Are we on the brink of unlocking a power that could reshape the very foundations of our world, or are we merely scratching the surface of a more profound mystery that has yet to reveal itself?

The Subzero Veil, with its ethereal connotations of frost and shadow, whispers of realms beyond our understanding, realms where time and space intertwine in ways we can scarcely imagine. Could this veil be a gateway to parallel dimensions, alternate realities, or even the realm of the gods themselves? As we stand on the precipice of the unknown, gazing into the icy abyss that lies beyond the Ice Wall, we cannot help but wonder what otherworldly beings or cosmic forces await us in the depths of this frozen enigma.

- Unveiling the Lexicon of Secrets

In the dimly lit chambers of ancient civilizations, a whispered language echoes through the corridors of time. The Lexicon of Secrets, a cryptic collection of words and symbols, holds the key to unlocking hidden knowledge and unraveling the mysteries of the universe.

Words inscribed on weathered tablets tell of forgotten realms and arcane powers long lost to the annals of history. Runes carved into stone murals depict scenes of cosmic significance, hinting at a deeper understanding of the world beyond our perception.

Scholars and scribes throughout the ages have sought to decipher the enigmatic language of the Lexicon, piecing together fragments of wisdom scattered across the ages: each word, each symbol, a clue to the more extraordinary tapestry of existence waiting to be unveiled.

As the intrepid explorer delves deeper into the Lexicon's secrets, a sense of awe and reverence fills their heart. The mysteries contained within these ancient texts transcend the boundaries of time and space, connecting past, present, and future in a seamless continuum of knowledge.

Through the whispers of the Lexicon, hidden truths are revealed, casting light on the shadows of ignorance and guiding the seeker toward enlightenment. The language of the ancient sages speaks not only of the past but also of the infinite possibilities that lie ahead, waiting to be discovered by those brave enough to seek them out.

In the hallowed halls where the Lexicon of Secrets lives, the air is thick with the weight of ages past. Each word uttered reverberates through the corridors of time, echoing the wisdom of the ancients and stirring the seeker's soul to new heights of understanding.

As the pages of the Lexicon turn, unveiling mysteries long concealed, the reader is drawn into a world of magic and wonder, where the unseen language becomes the key to unlocking the secrets of the universe. In this realm of hidden truths and whispered knowledge, the true power of the Lexicon is revealed: to awaken the seeker to the infinite possibilities that lie just beyond the veil of perception.

Now consumed by a hunger for knowledge that cannot be satiated, the seeker feels a pull toward the center of the ancient chamber where the Lexicon rests. As they approach, a subtle hum fills the air, resonating with the cosmos' heartbeat. The symbols etched upon the Lexicon's aged cover seem to shimmer and dance, beckoning the seeker closer.

With trembling hands, the seeker opens the Lexicon, bathed in a soft, ethereal glow that seems to emanate from within its pages. The words leap off the parchment, pulsing with a life force transcending mere language, reaching out to touch the deepest recesses of the seeker's soul.

As the seeker reads, a sense of profound connection washes over them, as if they are tapping into a source of knowledge that has long been waiting to be revealed. Words of power and wisdom flow through their minds, weaving a tapestry of understanding that expands their consciousness and redefines their existence.

The seeker loses track of time and space in the Lexicon's embrace's secrets, drifting through a realm of pure thought and pure being. They realize the Lexicon is not just a book of words but a doorway to infinite possibilities, a portal to realms beyond the known universe where truth and wisdom reign supreme.

And so, the seeker continues to delve deeper into the mysteries of the Lexicon, their quest for enlightenment driving them forward on a journey of discovery that will forever change the course of their life and the fate of the universe itself.

- Deciphering the Ice Wall's Tongue

Throughout centuries, the Ice Wall has remained an enigmatic entity, shrouded in mystery and intrigue. Its icy facade conceals physical barriers and a language of its own—a language of symbols and signals that speak to those willing to listen.

Deciphering the Ice Wall's tongue is no easy feat. It requires a keen eye, a sharp mind, and a deep reverence for the unknown. The ice whispers secrets of the ancient past, of forgotten civilizations and alien encounters. It weaves a tapestry of history and myth, drawing those who dare to unravel its mysteries deeper into its frozen embrace.

For centuries, explorers and scientists have sought to decode the language of the Ice Wall to understand its messages and meanings. Some believe that it holds the key to unlocking profound truths about our world and the universe beyond. Others see it as a gateway to realms unseen, a portal to dimensions beyond our comprehension.

But the Ice Wall's tongue is not easily tamed. It resists simple translation, dancing on the edge of understanding, teasing with glimpses of insight before retreating into the icy silence. Those who listen closely may hear echoes of ancient wisdom, of cosmic truths whispered across the frozen expanse.

In deciphering the Ice Wall's tongue, one must be prepared for wondrous and unsettling revelations. It is a journey into the heart of mystery, a quest for knowledge that may forever alter our perception of reality. The language of the Ice Wall is not just a means of communication—it is a doorway to the unknown, a pathway to the infinite realms that lie beyond the icy veil.

As we strive to unravel the secrets of the Ice Wall, we remember that its tongue speaks not just of frost and snow but of boundless possibility and unfathomable wonder. In listening to its whispers, we may find ourselves transformed; our understanding expanded beyond the confines of our earthly existence. The language of the Ice Wall is a riddle waiting to be solved, a puzzle that may hold the key to unlocking the universe's greatest mysteries.

The symbols etched into the icy surface of the Ice Wall seem to shift and shimmer with an otherworldly glow, hinting at a deeper connection to forces beyond our understanding. Some ancient texts suggest that the Ice Wall was not always a barrier, but a bridge between worlds–a conduit for beings of great power to traverse the cosmos.

Legends speak of a time when the Ice Wall was a focal point for interstellar travelers, a meeting place for celestial beings and earthly mortals to exchange knowledge and wisdom. The language of the Ice Wall was said to reflect this cosmic dialogue, a blend of starlight and earthly elements that bound the fabric of existence.

As we gaze upon the frozen expanse of the Ice Wall, we cannot help but feel a sense of awe and reverence for its silent majesty. It stands as a testament to the enduring mysteries of our world, a sentinel watching over the eons with a stoic presence that both beckons and repels.

The language of the Ice Wall remains a challenge and a promise, a riddle waiting to be unraveled by those bold enough to venture into its icy depths. Will we unlock its secrets and usher in a new era of understanding, or will the language of the Ice Wall remain a tantalizing enigma forever beyond our grasp? The answers lie hidden within the frozen realm, awaiting those with the courage to seek them out.

Index of Unseen Realms

As readers delve further into the shadowy corridors of mystery within the Index of Unseen Realms, they are drawn into a labyrinthine web of interconnected truths and hidden meanings that transcend the boundaries of conventional understanding. The frozen frontier of the unknown stretches endlessly before them, a boundless expanse of enigmatic secrets waiting to be unraveled.

Time becomes a fluid and elusive concept within the depths of the Index, twisting and turning with an otherworldly grace that defies human comprehension. Echoes of forgotten epochs reverberate through the ice, whispering tales of long-lost civilizations and ancient wonders that once flourished in the hidden corners of the unfathomable expanse. Each page turn reveals an additional layer of the cosmic tapestry, weaving together the disparate threads of reality into a grand symphony of existence that resonates across the eons.

The primal forces that shape the very fabric of reality come alive within the pages of the Index, pulsing with an undeniable power that transcends mortal understanding. Creation and destruction dance in an eternal cosmic ballet, their interplay shaping the essence of existence in ways that defy logic and reason. As readers immerse themselves in the enigmatic depths of the unseen realms, they are confronted with profound truths that challenge the very nature of reality itself.

Prophecies and ancient lore converge within the pages of the Index, offering glimpses into a greater truth that lies hidden beneath the icy surface of the unknown. The shadows of the ice wall conceal secrets and revelations that have eluded the grasp of mortal minds for eons, beckoning readers to venture deeper into the mysterious expanse and embrace the boundless possibilities that await in the uncharted depths.

Through the ethereal lens of the Index, readers are granted a fleeting glimpse into the vast unknown, a tantalizing hint of the infinite mysteries that lie beyond the veil of perception. It is a portal to the ineffable, a gateway to the realms of existence that defy explanation and challenge the very foundations of reality itself. As readers venture further into the enigmatic tapestry of the unseen realms, they are urged to cast aside their preconceptions and open their minds to the profound truths that await in the shadows of the ice wall.

- Navigating the Enigmatic Extents

Navigating the enigmatic extends beyond the Ice Wall and demands a transcendent connection to the elements and a profound understanding of the cosmic forces at play. As adventurers set forth into this uncharted realm, they are surrounded by a palpable sense of mystery and wonder that permeates the very fabric of existence.

The ethereal dance of the Northern Lights above casts a mesmerizing glow upon the icy landscape, illuminating the path ahead like a beacon of otherworldly guidance. The pulsating emerald, crimson, and indigo hues seem to whisper ancient secrets to those who are aware to listen.

Amidst the frozen expanse, the region's magnetic anomalies create a disorienting kaleidoscope of energies that challenges the very essence of navigation. Compass needles quiver and gyrate, pointing in erratic directions, while time itself seems to ebb and flow like a cosmic tide. Only those with a deep connection to the subtle vibrations of the Earth's magnetic field can hope to maintain their bearings amidst the swirling maelstrom.

Yet, beyond the physical challenges lie the metaphysical depths of the Ice Wall—an enigmatic gateway to realms beyond comprehension. Whispers of long-forgotten civilizations echo through the icy winds, hinting at a profound tapestry of hidden knowledge and cosmic truths waiting to be unveiled by the intrepid seeker.

Legends speak of ancient cities ensconced beneath the frozen layers, their spires reaching towards the heavens like forgotten dreams of a bygone era. It is said that within these icy citadels lie artifacts of unimaginable power and wisdom, relics of a time when the boundaries between worlds were blurred and the veil of reality was thin.

Navigating these enigmatic extents is to embark on a journey of self-discovery and transformation—a quest for enlightenment that transcends the limitations of the mundane world. Each step brings the voyager closer to the heart of the cosmic mystery, drawing them inexorably toward a revelation that will forever alter their perception of reality.

As the winds whisper secrets of ages past and the ice murmurs tales of forgotten realms, those who dare to venture beyond the Ice Wall find themselves on the threshold of a profound awakening—a journey of the soul that transcends time and space, leading them towards the ultimate truth that lies shrouded in the icy depths of the unknown.

- Guiding Through the Shadows

As they pressed deeper into the shadows beyond the Ice Wall, the explorers felt a tangible shift in the very fabric of reality. The air grew colder, clinging to their skin like a ghostly embrace, while whispers of long-forgotten languages brushed against their ears, leaving a shiver down their spines.

The landscape morphed before their eyes, twisting and contorting into surreal shapes and forms that defied logic and reason. They navigated through a labyrinth of shadowy corridors and winding pathways, each step leading them further into the heart of mystery.

The ancient ice murmured secrets of bygone civilizations, its frozen surface bearing traces of forgotten runes and symbols that seemed to pulse with their own life. The explorers felt a profound reverence and humility in the presence of such ancient knowledge, realizing that they were fleeting visitors in a realm long before their time.

As they delved more deeply, the shadows seemed to take on a life of their own, fusing into ethereal shapes that hovered just beyond the reach of their outstretched hands. Whispers of prophecy and revelation echoed through the icy corridors, hinting at a destiny intertwined with the essence of the cosmos.

The explorers felt a surge of awe and wonder at the vastness of the secrets concealed within the shadows beyond the Ice Wall. Each revelation sparked a thirst for deeper understanding, a hunger to unravel the enigmas hidden in the veils of time and space.

Guided by the flickering light of their lanterns and the whispers of the shadows, the explorers forged ahead, their hearts beating in harmony with the pulse of the unknown. In the shadows lay answers to their questions and a profound connection to the infinite tapestry of existence, woven with threads of light and darkness, mystery and revelation.

The explorers soon came upon a chamber bathed in an eerie blue light emanating from a towering crystal at its center. As they drew closer, they felt a powerful energy pulsating from the crystal, resonating with the very essence of their beings. Symbols danced upon its surface, shifting and rearranging in a hypnotic display that seemed to beckon them closer.

At that moment, an ancient and resonant voice echoed through the chamber, speaking in a language that transcended words. It spoke of cosmic cycles and celestial alignments, of forgotten realms and lost civilizations, weaving a tapestry of knowledge that spanned the depths of time.

The explorers stood transfixed, enveloped in the wisdom of the ages, as the crystal bathed them in its ethereal glow. They understood then that they were standing at the threshold of something greater than themselves, a gateway to realms beyond the limits of human comprehension.

With hearts open to the mysteries of the cosmos, the explorers took a collective breath and stepped forward, ready to embrace the unknown and unlock the secrets buried within the shadows beyond the Ice Wall.

- Illuminating the Darkened Ice

As explorers ventured further beyond the Ice Wall, they found themselves enveloped in a realm of eerie stillness and majestic beauty. The vast expanse of frozen landscape stretched out before them, a pristine canvas of ice and snow that seemed to whisper tales of ages long past. Amid this frozen wilderness, a sense of awe and wonder gripped their hearts as if they were standing on the threshold of a realm untouched by time.

As they ventured deeper into the icy realm, the explorers uncovered signs of a lost civilization that had once thrived in these frigid lands. Ancient structures lay buried beneath layers of frost, their intricate designs hinting at a sophistication that defied the harsh environment. Symbols etched into the ice walls spoke of a language long forgotten, of rituals and knowledge that had been preserved in the frozen silence.

Strange and otherworldly creatures lurked in the shadows, their eyes gleaming with an uncanny intelligence that seemed to transcend mere earthly existence. The explorers watched in amazement as these beings moved effortlessly through the icy terrain, their presence evoking a sense of reverence and trepidation.

Whispers of a gateway to another world lingered in the icy air, beckoning the explorers to unravel the mysteries that lay beyond the frozen veil. They felt a pull, a deep-seated curiosity that urged them to push further into the unknown, to seek the truths that lay hidden amidst the chill and darkness.

With each step forward, the explorers delved deeper into the heart of the Ice Wall, their minds buzzing with a mixture of fear and fascination. They knew they were on the brink of a discovery that would shake the foundations of their understanding of the world, of existence itself.

And then, as they rounded a corner in the icy expanse, they beheld a sight that took their breath away. A radiant light pierced through the darkness, illuminating a chamber of incredible beauty and complexity. The walls were adorned with intricate carvings and shimmering crystals, casting a mesmerizing glow that spoke of a hidden power waiting to be unleashed.

In that moment, the explorers felt a surge of anticipation and wonder, knowing that they were about to uncover a truth that had long been shrouded in mystery. The journey beyond the Ice Wall had led them to this pivotal moment, where the secrets of the frozen realm would be revealed in all their awe-inspiring splendor.

About the Author

Cassiel E. Nox is a renowned writer whose works transcend the boundaries of science, mystery, and imagination. Known for developing intricate tales, these stories merge conspiracy theories, metaphysics, and the latest discoveries in quantum physics. The science fiction narratives are both captivating and thought-provoking. With a passion for exploring the hidden mysteries of the universe, the writing delves deep into subjects such as extraterrestrial life, ancient secret knowledge, and cryptic phenomena. Cassiel's storytelling prowess is apparent in "Hidden Depths: The Kincaid Conspiracy and The Secrets of The Grand Canyon" and "Beyond The Collider: CERN's Quantum Rift And The Mandela Effect Mystery." In these stories, the intersections of scientific experiments and anomalous collective memories, often called the Mandela Effect, are not just brought to life, but they captivate the reader, holding their attention from start to finish. The journey continues with "From Roswell to Today: The Timeline of UFOs and Aliens," an exciting exploration of historical and contemporary accounts of UFO sightings and extraterrestrial phenomena. Cassiel is working on a science-fiction series called "When Something is Nothing," which promises to expand the horizons of imagination and intrigue further. Venturing into the world of science fiction, Cassiel crafts narratives that transport readers to distant stars and futuristic societies, all while grounded in scientific plausibility and human experience. With a background steeped in academic research and a passion for unraveling conspiracies, Cassiel E. Nox remains a distinctive voice in speculative fiction, inviting audiences to question the boundaries of reality and dream beyond the known.

Read more at https://my.ionos.com/domain-details/ quantumwriterverse.com.